Víctor CATALÀ (Caterina ALBERT I PARADÍS, 1869-1966) was born in the small fishing community of L'Escala into a landowning family. At twenty-one she became the effective head of the family on the death of her father, a lawyer and Catalan political activist. Besides caring for a younger brother and sister, she nursed her invalid mother and grandmother in a life of almost complete physical and social isolation.

By the turn of the century, the poetry and stories of Caterina Albert i Paradís had already gained prominence under her pseudonym of Víctor Català. Her female identity was revealed only in 1902, when she was thirty-three, around the time that her collection of short stories, *Drames Rurals* (*Rural Dramas*) was published.

Shortly afterward she was commissioned to write a novel for serial publication in the magazine *Joventut* (*Youth*). *Solitude* first appeared in four installments between May 1904 and April 1905.

D1229798

SOLITUDE

a novel by
Víctor Català

(Caterina Albert
i Paradís)

**translated from the Catalan
with a Preface by
David H. Rosenthal**

*with the Author's Foreword
to the Fifth Edition*

readers international

Wingate College Library

The title of this book in Catalan is *Solitud*, first published in book form in Barcelona in 1905.
Copyright © 1966 Estate of Caterina Albert i Paradís

First published in English by Readers International Inc., Columbia Louisiana and Readers International, London. Editorial inquiries to the London office at 8 Strathray Gardens, London NW3 4NY England. US/Canadian inquiries to the Subscriber Service Department, P.O.Box 959, Columbia LA 71418-0959 USA.
English translation copyright © 1992 Readers International Inc.
All rights reserved

The editors wish to thank the Institució de les Lletres Catalanes and the Arts Council of Great Britain for their support. The editors also wish to thank Julie Flanagan, who translated the *Author's Foreword to the Fifth Edition*.

Cover illustration: *The Farmer's Wife* (1922-23) by Joan Miró, courtesy of the Fundació Joan Miró, Barcelona.
Cover design by Jan Brychta.
Printed and bound in Malta by Interprint Ltd.

Library of Congress Catalog Card Number: 92-64284
Cataloguing-in-Publication Data: A catalogue record for this book is available from the British Library.

ISBN 0-930523-91-1 Hardcover
ISBN 0-930523-92-X Paperback

Contents

Contents

Preface

Caterina Albert i Paradís (1869-1966), all of whose work appeared under the patriotic masculine pen name Víctor Català, is considered one of Catalonia's greatest novelists. Born in L'Escala, a fishing village near both the French border and the ancient Greek settlement at Empúries, she began writing songs and poems secretly as a little girl, but it was not until 1901 that she published her first book, *El cant dels mesos (Song of the Months)*. By 1905, when *Solitude* appeared, she had also brought forth three volumes of short stories and was ranked among her nation's leading authors.

Solitude, however, which might have been the beginning of Víctor Català's career as a writer at the peak of her powers, proved also to be its end. Though she published another half-dozen books in the following sixty years, none was well received by critics or readers, and today her reputation still rests mainly upon her work between 1900 and 1905. Naturally, one would like to know what went wrong, but the evidence is slim and one can only guess at the reasons for her prolonged silences and gradual withdrawal from public life – not to mention her reluctance to enter it in the first place, which prevented her from claiming the literary prizes her early work had won her.

Solitude itself, that combined masterpiece and swan song, is as mysterious a book as its author. Mila, the young heroine, is taken by her husband Matias to live in an isolated hermitage high in the Pyrenees. There she meets the shepherd Gaietà, a storyteller for whom the mountains are full of strange and beautiful legends, and Anima, a bestial figure who lures Matias into a life of gambling, murders Gaietà, and finally rapes Mila. In one sense, the novel tells the story of an adolescent girl growing into womanhood, discovering her own emotional depths and needs, the violent and sinister realities that surround her, and the stolid male indifference that leads her ultimately to quit her shadowy, abulic husband and threaten to kill him if he follows her. But this journey to self-knowledge takes place in a landscape so symbolically charged and peopled that we're constantly adjusting our perspectives as we make our way through it − or to put the matter differently, the realism, as in other great early twentieth-century novels, is psychological rather than external. Gaietà, that embodiment of the creative imagination, and Anima, that menacing presence, are far less ambiguously drawn than Mila, who appears as a real woman played off against a pair of primordial symbols through whom she comes to define her own vision of the world.

In this Gaietà acts as her teacher, rescuing her from a nervous breakdown and encouraging her to see the mountains as he sees them:

> Forcing her to gaze over every steep precipice, teaching her how to twist her body and secure her footing in dangerous spots, making her look down when they were halfway up a cliff and laughing at her terror, he helped conquer her fears, held her when she was dizzy, and guided the woman through her mountain apprenticeship, winning out at last over her timorous, fawn-like nature. And now she loved the excitement she felt on those peaks and the way the yawning depths seemed to suck her soul out of her.

By being her friend, Gaietà also steers her away from stock solutions to her problems, which he refuses to let her forget in his arms. He thus helps Mila to earn her maturity without a man's support or domination, while height and isolation force her to live within herself.

In addition, the Pyrenees themselves play a major role in *Solitude*, sometimes as a realm of female landscapes (a notion reinforced by Gaietà's story of the old celibate who falls in love with the beautiful fairy Dawnflower) that mirror the heroine's aroused longings, and sometimes as a cruel place of sudden death and male predation (also underlined by the shepherd's tale of the girl seduced and abandoned by the Lord of Llisquents). The vivid descriptions of the changing seasons, and the way the natural world both mirrors and provokes Mila's own shifting moods, contribute greatly to the book's lyric power:

The first glimmers of daylight seemed to materialize imperceptibly in tiny particles, and their very pallor, more than the dark, filled the grove with ominous shapes, whose blurred outlines and proportions made everything as fantastic as Gaietà's stories. Mila turned her head from side to side, prey to an irrational fear that had tormented her as a girl. Sometimes she felt she was walking on air, and sometimes every cranny or patch of brambles concealed a skeletal hand that would tug at her skirts. And the pines, those bizarre silhouettes huddled together in clumps, seemed like evil apparitions that watched her pass and then wickedly stole after her.

For such poetic intensity, mythic richness, and psychological insight, *Solitude* deserves to be listed with the great novels of its era. That it has never been translated into English (though versions have appeared in other languages) is primarily due to the fact that it was written in Catalan, a language that has suffered more than its share of vicissitudes in this century. At the time of *Solitude*'s publication, Catalan literature (which had produced some of Europe's finest medieval and Renaissance work, including Joanot Martorell's *Tirant lo Blanc*, described by Cervantes as "the best book in the world") had recently emerged from a three-hundred-year decline. In the late nineteenth and early twentieth centuries, however, Catalan authors made up for lost time and reestablished their nation as a center of literary activity. This period, which culminated in the Spanish Republic, ended abruptly with Franco's victory in 1939. Catalan culture was then brutally repressed for twenty years and benignly neglected for fifteen more, thus making the literature almost inaccessible to interested foreigners.

Since Franco's death, Catalans have moved steadily toward self-rule. They now have a bilingual government and a Statute of Autonomy. The study of Catalan is obligatory in the schools, and Catalan daily newspapers and television channels are free to operate for the first time since 1939. One hopes that authors like Víctor Català will now also begin to receive the recognition they deserve in the English-speaking world, and that *Solitude*, a book unique in its vision of the inner life of an ordinary Mediterranean woman, will assume its rightful place among Europe's great early modern novels.

David H. Rosenthal

Author's Foreword
to the Fifth Edition of *Solitude**

When the illustrious Director of the magazine *Joventut* [Lluís Via], mouthpiece of literary controversies at the beginning of this century, requested a book from me as part of his plan for the simultaneous publication of four supplements, I asked if he might not prefer a collection of stories to a novel. He promptly replied that, if he had the choice, a novel would be better because he already had the promise of a volume of stories from Mestre Ruyra [Joaquim Ruyra, 1858-1939].

At the appearance not long before of my *Drames Rurals*, some of its critics had accused me of excessive concentration on the dramatic element and of squeezing too much into too little space. I also recognized that, out of fear of losing the reader's interest, I tended to eliminate details, to strip verbiage too zealously from the body of my stories. Thus I responded to the kind suggestion of *Joventut* by considering another rural drama, this time not restricting flights of fancy, not stinting description in a work that would not be unduly schematic. Since I like even figures more than odd ones, I planned the novel around twenty chapters, their scope and length demanded by their subject matter.

---

*This statement and edition of *Solitude* did not appear until 1945. A November 1937 Prologue by Lluís Via indicates that an earlier publication of *Solitude* was interrupted by the Spanish Civil War of 1936-1939. The *Foreword* has been translated by Julie Flanagan.

I began the task according to this initial idea. My optimism and confidence were to miscarry, however, because the pen soon started to have its own way, filling page after page, with distressing prodigality. In effect, with this extraordinary redoubled outpouring, the details to be captured multiplied, concepts split into new concepts, sentences bifurcated luxuriantly into unlooked-for densities...

This density, this prodigality, appalled me and once again I began to fear excess... Once more it became a question of paring, of setting limits. I did not have the heart to disturb arbitrarily the general structure of the novel, but was determined to lessen the density of the whole, to ease the compression. As I was unable to go back and reorganize it all again (I was writing and simultaneously sending the original off to the printer for immediate publication), I chose to sacrifice two entire chapters, those which seemed least essential in the unfolding of the story. *Solitude* thus consists of eighteen chapters instead of the original twenty I wanted for it.

It appeared in this form and went into several printings until, when yet another was on the point of coming out, I was speaking to Lluís Via about the amputated sections which were unknown to him as to everyone else. This good friend was greatly concerned that they should be reintegrated, and he referred to them in his magnificent Prologue.

However, the fratricidal war, which wrecked so many things with its obstacles and unforeseen upheavals, paralyzed publication temporarily, and when I returned home, it was to a disagreeable surprise. This was occasioned under the curious pretext of...a search for weapons! A register carried out by clumsy hands, guided by an appropriate intelligence, had turned the whole house upside-down. Clothes thrown out of wardrobes made fodder for moths, and papers taken from shelves and drawers lay scattered in utmost confusion over the floor, tables and chairs.

The focus of the offence had disappeared – my great-grandfather's shotgun, which had helped repel the invader during the *guerra del francès* [Spanish resistance to Napoleon, 1808-1814], plus the sabre of a general who had participated in the glorious African campaign of 1859. With these two relics and a handful of French francs, scant remains of excursions to our neighbor Republic, also vanished the two unpublished chapters of *Solitude*. For all my searching and rummaging about, no more than a few scattered pages were found in the unlikeliest places, and these pages contain the fragment now about to make its first appearance, not because I believe that it has any particular merit, or that it is needed by the novel, but as a small anecdotal detail, a witness respecting the intention and express desire of a great, now-lost friend whose memory has always earned my highest esteem.

Solitude

I. The Ascent

After passing through Ridorta, they had come across a wagon going their way and Matias, who wanted to preserve his strength, asked the driver if he would mind taking them as far as the foot of the mountain. The peasant, beaming at the prospect of a little conversation, made room for the man by his side and told Mila to make herself comfortable on the straw mats at the back. She looked gratefully at that unknown benefactor, for though strong, she was exhausted. Her husband had said the trip from Llisquents, where the delivery man had left them, to Ridorta would take less than half an hour, but they had been walking at least an hour and a quarter when they saw the town's blackened steeple rising above the green hill. Another fifteen minutes passed before they saw the wagon, and what with the sun, the dust, and the rough dirt road, the poor woman had fallen into a very bad temper.

Once settled, with her back to the man and her bundle of clothes beside her, she untied the kerchief around her head and, taking the ends in her hands, beat it to fan her face. She was hot, and the cool breeze flowed over her temples and neck like a gentle though slightly unnerving caress. When she stopped fanning herself, she felt calmer and ready to look at the pretty sights Matias had so often described.

She gazed from side to side. Behind them, the road twisted and turned, full of holes, tracks, and caked, muddy ridges the wagon wheels wore down with such excruciating slowness that they would not be level till the middle of summer. Then the road would become a sea of dust till the autumn rains returned.

On the left was a high embankment that jutted out at the top, as though about to cave in onto the road, but it was held back by rough, uneven walls that bulged here and there and were more dangerous than the embankment itself. Above them were fields enclosed by rows of magueys, whose stiff, fleshy leaves slashed the air like bouquets of swords, and, in some places, by swaying tamarisks and rows of buckthorn, whose white blossoms, girded by thorns, had just begun to flower.

On the other side, starting a couple of yards from the road, the Ridorta plain began, hugging the base of the hill and divided into small symmetrical patches that looked like a big checkerboard. Those irrigated fields were the town's riches, subdivided among its inhabitants by ancient feudal contracts. The brilliant colors of sprouting vegetables dotted the scorched brown earth, among ditches whose water glistened in the sunlight like bright strips of mirror.

Mila was dazzled by such lushness. A child of the lowland plains, barren for want of hands, water, and fertilizer, she started incredulously at what seemed a fantastic mirage: that other little plain which, nestled between a hillside covered with houses and several harsh, stony mountains, nourished this fertile and joyous existence. Not one square foot wasted, not one weed stealing the earth's goodness! Everything tilled, everything turned upside down by hoes and pitchforks, everything pampered like a lord, everything proudly blossoming with abundant generosity!

Down below, in Mila's country, the people were scattered through the land, with great stretches between them. Among thick hedges of bug-infested bushes, green lizards flashed in the sun and a few emaciated cows, whose ribs stuck out like bars and whose anklebones were so sharp they nearly pierced the hide, tugged at the few dry weeds. Here no such useless beast could be seen, and the people were as close-set as fingers on a hand: a crowd of women, clustered like chessmen on a board, swarmed like industrious ants across the fields, raking the earth, raising and lowering the chain pump, heaping soil around the vegetables or resting in the shade of a fig tree, all with their skirts hiked up, kerchiefs on their heads, and bare arms and legs, tan and healthy in the sun.

As she gazed upon them, Mila's farmgirl soul filled with an urge, a wistful longing to leap from the wagon, run into the fields and, like those women, plunge her hands into the warm earth, the wet leaves, the water flowing between rushes, whose yellow flowers nodded gravely beside the irrigation ditches.

Matias had been right: Ridorta was a cheerful place, a town perched upon a hill and ringed by fields. And if the district was so happy, the hermitage above it couldn't be as gloomy as she had heard. Mila imagined it as a little nest where, as soon as she stuck her head out the window, she would gaze down upon this marvelous vista. Oh, if she could only clear her own little garden and plant it as she liked, she would never regret having to leave her village forever!

Excited by these thoughts, she turned to share them with her husband, but at the sight of those two backs, the words died in her throat and the hopeful idea that had been about to venture forth scurried back into its lair like a frightened animal.

The two men spoke slowly, without noticing her, and she half-caught the words: "Cold...gloomy...calves...too high," but she never learned what they were talking about because her thoughts fled back to the fields. The spell, however, had been broken, and the land, just as beautiful as it had been a moment ago, could not rekindle her first enthusiasm. She sadly turned and looked upward: the sky, vast and empty, blazed with blinding light that hurt her eyes. She peered through the crack between the two men: there was something uniformly green in the distance, like a splendid carpet... She looked again at the two backs: one, the peasant's, slender and bony like those cows in her district, was clad in a cheap shirt, worn thin by many washings, that smelled of sweat and charcoal dust. The other back, broad and soft as a pillow, strained against the black jacket that stretched from armpit to armpit, as if in constant danger of ripping asunder.

"How fat he's gotten since we married," thought Mila, remembering how tight all his clothes had become, so that he seemed crammed into them like a straw doll in its rags. The felt hat that had previously suited him so well had gradually come to look like a priest's calotte, and his ears, which stuck out on either side, were red and translucent like tinted glass. The crease on his starched collar, set against the black jacket and folds of flesh, had the icy pallor of marble.

The two men's shadows fell across Mila like a cool mantle, and she felt snug and happy curled up in her straw nest.

The wagon, meanwhile, advanced slowly, so slowly that one might have thought it merely swayed from side to side with no other mission than to flatten the caked dirt on the road. From the time she saw a tree to the time they passed it, one could have calmly said part of a rosary; and that parsimonious rocking filled her with drowsiness.

She was tired of looking at their backs, the sky, and the patchwork colors of the fields, and her neck ached from twisting her head so long. She rubbed it to smooth out that painful stiffness and, after seeking a comfortable posture, she remained motionless, her back against the wagon's side as she admired the mat in front of her: a lovely mat that resembled a thick silk net, sprinkled with gold stars which sparkled in the sunlight. Overcome by that sweet languor, she saw a red curtain, then a blue one, and then a black one...

A slap on the back woke her with a start.

"What is it?" she mumbled sleepily.

"Come on, time to get off!" replied her husband, standing on the wagon, which had stopped.

She pulled herself together, swayed to her feet, and they jumped down.

"So long, friend, and God bless you."

"So long, hermit, and thanks for the company. See you on St. Pontius' Day."

"Come by and have a drink."

"Sure... Bye now."

"Goodbye."

The peasant's face, bright red like the bottom of a stewpot on the fire, burst into a broad smile. He pulled in the reins as if they were made of rubber, calmly cried "Giddyup!" a few times...and the wagon slowly moved forward, leaving husband and wife behind, backed against the dry roadside wall with a dazed expression on their faces.

"Did you hear that?" asked the woman. "He called you hermit."

"Because I told him we were going to look after the hermitage."

"It gives me a headache..." she added, gazing vaguely into the distance.

"What does?"

"All this...you know what I mean... A young man shouldn't do a job that's meant for someone old and sickly."

"Don't be silly! One job's as good as another."

And the man began stamping his feet to shake down his trousers, which had ridden up on his legs in the course of their journey.

With a sigh, Mila also smoothed her skirts.

When his pantlegs once again reached his ankles, Matias pushed a stick through his kerchief, in which he had bundled a few articles of clothing, and hoisted it onto his shoulder.

"Well, are you ready?"

She gripped the bundle under her arm.

"Let's go."

A little further along, there was a break in the roadside wall where a sort of path began. It was a deep, uneven gully, carpeted with smooth, loose stones: one of many gashes in the mountain's huge rocky face, down which the sky's abundant tears flowed during winter storms.

They set out again single file, he whistling between his teeth and she turning around every few yards.

They hadn't gone more than fifty steps when she stopped.

"It's so steep!"

"They call it Legbreak Creek. It's dangerous in the winter."

"More than now?"

"This is nothing."

Seeing her worried look, he cheerfully added: "Wait'll you see Black Ravine! You really have to watch it there!"

"Are all the paths like this?"

"These are shortcuts, woman. The real path starts further up, after Murons, but the shortcuts are handier. You aren't used to it yet, but after a while you'll like going this way. See what I mean? Going up is worse than climbing stairs, but coming down is easy. Like swinging on a rope: your feet can't stop, and before you know, it's over."

She sighed, and then started walking again. Her feet kept dislodging stones, and the brambles stuck to her clothes like handfuls of barbed hooks.

He gradually stopped whistling, while her bundle began to weigh on her like a boulder. Fifty steps further, she sat down to rest.

Matias, who led the way, turned around.

"What, again?"

"I've got to...rest."

"We can't waste time. The sun'll set before we know it."

"Is it a long way to go?"

"Sure. We've just started!"

She sat up straight: "Holy Mary! We've been on the road since four this morning!"

He burst out laughing. "We just began climbing the mountain... Don't worry, we'll get there in time." And he turned to pluck a sprig of butcher's-broom from beside the path.

Mila then fixed her gaze upon him, a gaze full of worry and suspicion.

"Let's see if they were right to warn me that he'll make a fool of me again," she thought, rising to her feet.

He encouraged her: "Come on now. We'll be there in no time."

"If it weren't for this bundle! ..."

But Matias ignored the hint, and they walked on in silence. The gully became rockier and steeper. They kept slipping on the stones and had to grasp at the thickets to keep their footing. Their heavy breathing startled lizards, who frantically scurried for cover, and broom twigs whipped their flushed, sweaty faces. Matias had pushed back his felt hat, which now rested against his neck, and his starched collar had turned as soft as a piece of tripe.

The ground beside the path leveled from time to time as they approached an olive grove, but then the banks rose again, hemming them in so they could see only a strip of dazzling blue above their heads. In one grove they saw two oxen resting with their plow beneath an olive tree, while the plowman sat nearby, drinking from a black earthenware jug and grasping a large onion. The animals switched their tails and stamped to keep the flies away. The olive branches wove a filigreed silver arc against the sky, and the soil thrown up between the furrows made wide, brown stripes.

Mila gazed enviously at the peasant and mumbled: "If I dared, I'd ask him for a drink of water. My throat's dry as a bone!"

They approached him, drank, and talked for a short while. Matias again explained that they were on their way to the hermitage, and Mila again felt uneasy and ashamed without knowing why.

Then they continued their ascent, with those slippery stones beneath their feet, walking between banks of brambles and buckthorn that tore at them like the claws of some raging beast.

Matias coughed and a little bird, perched haughtily on a maguey, fled with a bright and piercing chirrup.

Despite the shadows across their path, the heat was stifling. Mila's wet blouse clung to her back, and her heart beat furiously.

The path suddenly swerved upward, as if to leap over some obstacle. Mila cried out in surprise at the light that bathed her body, though her legs remained submerged in the dark stream bed.

The gully branched off like an upside-down "Y": two branches flowed downhill, splitting apart with a great stretch of mountainside between them, while the third, a bit obliquely, continued upward. Where the three branches met, a small plateau had been carved out, as sunlit at that hour as the plain below them.

"We can rest here awhile," said Matias.

Mila didn't wait to be told twice and fell to earth, crushed and drained, with the blood pounding in her temples and the soles of her feet.

She looked at her shoes: ruined! They'd never be the same... And she thought that if he'd told her what the journey would really be like, she would have worn espadrilles and saved the shoes from their wedding...her only good pair.

To stifle her disappointment, she raised her head.

On the right, the gully descended as precipitously as a well. Mila crossed herself in thanks for having reached the top safely. That was a path for goats and bandits, not people.

On the far side of the gully, olive trees with cracked trunks dotted the slopes and cliffs; on the near side was a rocky field with some carob trees and flowering thyme, whose fragrance the wind carried toward them like an angel's pure breath.

The Y's left fork twisted and turned further, its end hidden in one of the mountain's many folds. And between the two branches, a rounded spur swelled like a woman's breast, made more realistic by its nipple: a bulge or natural menhir that marked off their plateau, outlined against the bright sky behind it. Just under the nipple, there were remnants of some Cyclopean steps and, above them, a rusted iron bolt had been driven into the rock.

"Do you know where we are?" Matias suddenly asked.

"How could I if I've never been here before?"

"Well, we're standing on Roquís Petit. There's three of them, you know: Roquís Gros, Roquís Mitjà in the middle, and this smaller one. That," and he pointed to the nipple, "is what they call the Moor's Boundary Stone. They say there used to be a Moorish king whose lookout sat here all day long. He couldn't sleep or move on pain of death."

"And where's the hermitage?"

"Down there, behind you, in back of that rock... Get up and I'll show you."

She rose listlessly to her feet, and he turned away from the plain and pointed southeast.

"On that dark mountain?"

"No, that's the Roquís Gros. Look closer. You see how Black Ravine winds around that ridged mountain like a bandage? Well, the ravine starts at St. Pontius' Pass, and underneath is the hermitage."

"Good God! We have to climb up there?"

"No, we'll take the first path we come to."

"Can you see those pretty fields from the hermitage?"

"From the hermitage itself...no. But from here you can see them."

Matias crossed the clearing and climbed to the top of the Boundary Stone. Mila wanted to do the same, but her legs wouldn't cooperate. Each step was four feet high.

"God, what steps!"

"The Moors built them... They say there used to be Moors all around here. Come on, give me your hands... Up you get! Now hold on here and look..."

Mila almost fainted. An immense void yawned before her, as if waiting to be filled, and only below, far below and far in the distance, stretched the tilled plain, like a wondrous residue of that golden spring evening. Ridorta, another large plain and many other villages nestled like turtledoves amidst dells, groves, and pathways. Her eyes lost the farthest ones in the hazy distance, in the horizon's misty blue.

The woman devoutly clasped her hands.

"How lovely it is!"

"Didn't I say you'd like it?" And he happily told her the names of all the towns and hills in sight.

Mila gazed in fascination, trying to take it all in and to engrave that magic scene in the depths of her retina. She would have forgotten to move if Matias hadn't laughed and, leaping from stone to stone, asked: "Haven't you had your fill?"

The question brought her back to earth. But before regretfully climbing down from the Boundary Stone, she allowed herself another lingering look.

The tail on the Y that led up the mountain wasn't as rough as the first gully, but their new path, without pebbles and carved into solid rock, was full of sharp angles that cut her feet more than the stones had.

Their weariness, which had led them to prolong their rest, now stifled any desire to chat. They climbed silently, with bowed heads, especially Mila who, hearing Matias' huffs and puffs ahead of her, thought how her husband's paunch was beginning to get in his way.

"But he doesn't care! He'll wind up looking like a whale!"

And for the first time she sensed that Matias, who seemed fresh as a daisy, would end up suffering from asthma.

This time Matias was the first to stop.

When she caught up, she shot him an angry glance and said: "If you'd told me the trip would take this long, I'd have brought something to eat... I'm worn out."

"Don't give up now! We're almost at the path to the hermitage."

"I know what you mean by *almost*," she replied sadly.

He didn't answer, and they started walking again.

But this time Matias had told the truth. A few minutes later they reached the path.

"Let's rest a little if you want to," he said.

"This is worse than Purgatory," was her only reply.

They sat down. Matias took out his tobacco pouch and rolled a cigarette. The woman took the kerchief off her head, shook it out and, since she was no longer hot, retied it around her neck.

They were halfway up Roquís Mitjà, which the setting sun stained red and orange above them, while below, the slope dropped steeply amid shadowy bluish crags and boulders.

There was no hint of a plain beneath them and the sky's pale gray stretched from side to side, flushed with orange toward the horizon, while mother-of-pearl clouds drifted slowly from left to right, changing shape and color. As Mila watched them absentmindedly, she noticed a black spot, like a fly that slowly grew bigger.

"What's that?" she asked Matias.

"It must be a raven."

"Now it's hovering over that side of the mountain..."

"Just above the Nina... It must smell something the people at St. Pontius threw in the ravine. There's a farmhouse below there."

"Why do they call it 'la Nina'?"

"Because from some places it looks like a girl's head with a little pigtail hanging down. Someday I'll show you the view above the Roar. At dawn it's blue as the sky and pretty as a picture."

Matias fell silent, his gaze lost in the distance, and Mila, seeing him so gentle and calm, thought that anyone would take him for a perfect saint. But suddenly, as if his mood had secretly goaded her, she turned away and shuddered.

With a cigarette between his lips, Matias led her down the path. It was narrow and smooth, as if a colossal wheel had rolled over it for centuries. It led southeast, and after a few steps they sighted the immense volcanic mass of Roquís Gros: an unchallenged sovereign shrouded in its mantle of blue-purple shadows that fell over caves and dells, lending them an imposing depth that took Mila's breath away.

From that mountain, still distant, flowed a wave of cold air, a strange wintry breeze that chilled skin warmed by the sun, filling Mila with such a strong urge to retreat that she stopped in her tracks. Then she heard a dull rumble coming from she didn't know where, like the snore of some sleeping monster.

"What's that noise, Matias?" she asked uneasily.

"That's the howl of Badblood Creek. It comes from the Roar."

Those words reminded Mila of everything her husband had told her about the miraculous waters that restored people's health, curing men and beasts of their woes and afflictions: scrofula, herpes, running sores, chronic diarrhea, eczema...

And while she was thinking about diseases and miracles, the path, climbing and twisting, led them around the mountain, penetrating deeper and deeper into its icy shadows.

Suddenly Mila halted and turned around, astounded: Holy Virgin, how far they'd traveled that day!

Beneath them, she saw nothing but waves of mountain, huge, silent mountains that sloped into the quiet dusk, which enveloped them in shadow like a darkening cloud.

Mila searched that blue emptiness for a wisp of smoke, a hut, a human figure... But she saw nothing, not the slightest indication that they shared that landscape with other human beings.

"How lonely!" she mumbled, stunned and feeling her spirit grow as dark or darker than those shady depths.

II. Darkness

As soon as they banged on one of the gates with a rock, a furious barking arose within the house, while other dogs barked back all around them.

Startled, Mila clutched her husband's arm, but he only laughed.

"Those are the fairies. They imitate everything they hear."

Mila felt even more terrified by that bizarre explanation, but before she could reply footsteps approached, muffled by the barking. A pale light shone above the wall topped with broken glass and nails. Something slid heavily across the gates, and after a moment of silence, a voice asked calmly: "Who goes there?"

"Open up, Gaietà. It's us."

"Who?"

"Me and my wife, Gaietà! Come on, open up."

There was another moment's silence.

"When'd you get here?" the voice within asked.

"Just now. My wife fell down on the way."

Still clutching her husband's arm, Mila whispered: "What's he waiting for?"

"He's suspicious...," Matias whispered back.

"What're you saying out there?" the voice asked.

"I'm telling my wife you're scared," and taking out his tobacco pouch, Matias laughed and added: "Look up, Gaietà. I'm throwing you my passport..." And he threw his pouch over the wall.

Then they heard a bolt being lifted, the sound of iron striking the earth, the creaking of a big key, and a golden crack appeared between the gates.

"Good evening," said Matias as he pushed.

"May God grant us all one..." And the gates opened all the way. They spied a small thin man with a gleaming sickle in his hand. Nearby a boy of about eight held a sooty lantern and the tobacco pouch.

Matias laughed when he saw the sickle.

"Ready for anything, eh, Gaietà?"

The little man laughed back.

"Might come in handy, y'know... I have to be on the lookout up here; there're more foxes than lambs."

He put down the sickle, which flashed menacingly in his hand, and then slammed the two gates shut with his knee, bolted them, fastened the bolt to a chain that hung from the wall, turned the big key in the lock, and, having done all this, calmly turned to face his guests, smiling again and rubbing his hands together.

"Now we can talk... I figured you'd get here around now... What's new?"

"New? We're dead on our feet..." Matias declared, and, taking his pouch from the boy's hand, he added, "We had no idea Baldiret was up here."

"You see, hermit, I get lonely all by myself in this big house, so I said to the boy: 'Come on up and keep me company,' and I tell him stories, you know..."

The man grinned at the lad, who looked back, grinned in return, and then blushingly hung his head.

Mila, who hadn't said a word beyond "Good evening," peered at everything around her. In the pale light from the lantern, she could barely make out a courtyard surrounded by the high walls of a house. In the middle, she saw a big glass bottle beside a well whose iron bucket was badly dented, while in the background a covered porch ran along the wall till it reached some stone steps that led down to the courtyard. She had no chance to see more because the man, still smiling and rubbing his hands together, turned to her and said: "Well, hermitess, he says you took a fall. What happened: did you get dizzy?"

"No. I tripped on a pine root; it's nothing." And Mila touched the gash on her forehead.

"It's still bleeding a bit, isn't it? But I don't think we'll need a priest. It'll soon be all right."

He turned to the boy, "Pick up that sickle, and let's go upstairs." And smiling once more at the couple, he added: "I bet you haven't eaten yet."

Matias told him how long it had been and, as they climbed the steps behind the boy, who carried the sickle and lantern, the little man explained that he'd cooked supper just in case.

"Hermitess, I don't know what you'll think of our food...unless you're good and hungry! We're terrible cooks, the boy and me..." and he laughed heartily.

He'd won Mila's heart, this kind and helpful man. He was short and skinny, but his figure seemed fleshed out by a loose jacket and dark, heavy woolen breeches. Half his face was covered by a wool cap, and the other half seemed more beardless than clean-shaven. She could hear the taps on his shoes as he walked calmly and deliberately. Mila reckoned he must be about forty years old.

Even if she hadn't known he was a shepherd, she would have guessed from the strong smell of sheep he gave off. The stench permeated the entire house. She'd noticed it before they knocked at the gate, it had grown stronger as they entered the courtyard, and now, inside the house where the breeze couldn't dissipate it, it became even stronger and more offensive.

They had walked along a terrace and entered the kitchen. It was a big room whose walls and ceiling, blackened by smoke and shadows, seemed to retreat from her gaze so that only the glint of copper and tin showed what kind of room they were in. Burning coals glowed in the fireplace, with something black beside them, perhaps a pot. With its four legs resting stiffly in the shadows, the long table resembled a headless beast about to charge the new arrivals.

Mila glimpsed a slippery stone sink, the doors of a cupboard, a flour sifter... But everything else remained mysterious, pregnant with surprises.

Still talking, the shepherd lit an oil lamp.

"Tonight you'll be strangers in your own home, and since the hermitess has never been in these parts we'll have to take her around, won't we? While you're setting the table, boy, I'll show her the house. Come on, hermitess..." But upon turning around and seeing her glance from side to side, he stopped: "You're not afraid of ghosts, are you? Fear's no good, a nasty little vermin. They say it especially bothers women, but we'll cure you here, God willing."

And he led her away. Mila looked around for Matias, but he'd stayed behind in the kitchen.

They entered another large room whose only furnishings were a grandfather clock, a couple of tables, and a few chairs. A heavy beam, resting on the wooden floor against the wall, looked like a dead serpent. At the sight of that drafty space, Mila shivered and recalled those lonely mountains shrouded in dark evening mist.

The shepherd told her that before, on the saint's day, people used to dance in this room, but now the floor was so weak that the *senyor* rector had forbidden it. One side of the room was windowless, the other had two doors, and there was a balcony at the far end.

"Let's look at your room first, hermitess."

There was a bed with a dark red cover, a writing desk, chairs and a wash basin. Gaietà's lamp was almost extinguished by a blast of cold air through the paneless window.

"Damn that mountain's stinking breath!"

The shepherd closed the shutters and, raising his lamp, showed her a framed print.

"St. Pontius, hermitess... A splendid saint, patron of good health."

The saint was dressed as a bishop, with a miter on his head and a crozier in his left hand. The other hand was held aloft, with two fingers extended in benediction.

They went on to the second room, where there was a bed, unmade this time, a wardrobe, a long table, and seven or eight wicker chairs. In one corner a winding staircase led upward, and in front of them another led down. Someone had tacked two scenes from St. Pontius' life to opposite walls: identical engravings that showed the holy martyr between two vases of flowers.

"Well, hermitess, that's your cage, big enough for a couple of birds and some nestlings too... Last time there were eight of them, between kids and grownups, and each one had his own nest... Now I'll show you the chapel. Believe me, it's a sight to see."

At that moment a sort of sonar flash suddenly zoomed over them, interrupting him and draining the color from her lips. Gaietà laughed so loud the flame on his lamp flickered.

"What a joke, hermitess! That gave you a fright?" Collecting himself a little, he added soothingly: "But you shouldn't get upset... It's just an owl that roosts upstairs in the belfry and wanted to say hello... Tomorrow we'll take a closer look at him; we'd never catch him now. And listen, don't be so jittery. I knew it as soon as I laid eyes on you, but you'll have to change if you want to stick around here. Otherwise you'll get sick. You see, people scare themselves. Believe me, Heaven and earth care mighty little about our doings."

But Mila, smiling to herself, remembered the flashing

sickle in the shepherd's hand and how cautiously he had opened the gates.

The floorboards creaked: it was Matias who approached, calling out: "Where are you? Where are you?"

He'd come to tell them the table was set and he was dying of hunger. Mila hurried after him, but Gaietà stopped her.

"Before sitting down, we have to visit the chapel. What'll the saint think if you snub him like that?" And he started down the staircase with the lamp in his hand.

Matias clucked in disapproval, but she smiled resignedly and followed their guide.

A powerful wave of stuffiness greeted them halfway down, and as they reached the bottom, a sepulchral chill like a damp sheet enfolded them. Mila shivered and hunched her shoulders.

At the end of the nave, straight and low-ceilinged as a railroad tunnel and equally dank, something gleamed dully like a distant star: it was the main altar.

Gaietà had stuck his woolen cap under his arm, and after crossing himself and showing Mila the font, he slowly advanced, knelt before the altar, and bowed his head. Then he rose again, lifted the lamp above his head, and moved it from side to side. Beneath the vault, surrounded by dirty gilding, by angels whose rosy flesh was covered with marks and scratches, by vases filled with twisted, dusty roses, Mila again spied St. Pontius with his tiny body, his bulging paunch, his long, ashy beard, his miter, his crozier in one hand and the other raised in benediction, and, as if a mighty storm were blowing, his clothes all rumpled. A long, pointed foot hung down, resembling Matias' tobacco pouch when it was empty. That was the third time she'd seen the saint within a few minutes, and he'd never seemed so ugly, with that tangled beard, that fat lady's belly, and that dangling foot which seemed superimposed upon his body. A strange sensation came over Mila, somewhere between revulsion and anguish, and she could not remember whether she'd finished the Paternoster she'd absentmindedly begun to recite.

That chapel full of terrors gave her goosebumps.

The shepherd would have happily shown her the whole place inch by inch, but in view of Matias' impatience he decided to let it ride.

"Some other time, hermitess...you'll see it all little by little." And showing her as they passed the strings of offerings hung on the walls – painted boards, arms and legs made of yellow wax, wooden croziers, long braids of discolored hair, all as stinking and worm-eaten as junk in an abandoned attic – he led them out through a little door behind the altar.

Mila breathed deeply, like someone who'd just escaped from prison. The door led to a sacristy full of old crates and broken tools, and the sacristy led to another room, also full of trash, dust, and cobwebs. As soon as they entered, they were assaulted by loud barks and scratching noises outside the far door.

Mila stepped backward, and Gaietà shouted: "Hey, Mussol, take it easy! Come on, boy, calm down." And he unbolted the door.

The dog leapt at the shepherd as if about to devour him.

"Don't back off, hermitess. There's nothing to be afraid of."

But the dog growled at the strangers, whereupon Gaietà grabbed its collar and buried its muzzle in the woman's skirts.

"What's this? Scolding the lady of the house? Take a good whiff, and if you do it again..."

He raised his hand, and the dog stopped growling.

They were in the shed where he kept his sheep. Its hot

stench was so strong that the woman held her breath, and she saw a vague whiteness before her, like snow on a dark night.

"This is my flock," said the shepherd. "A bunch of babes straight out of limbo... Tomorrow, I'll show you the saint's lambs: the prettiest of all."

At the other end of the shed, you could see the courtyard silhouetted against the pale starlight; a wooden fence kept the animals enclosed.

They crossed the shed, while the dog padded behind them. Mila's skirts weren't long enough to need raising, but every time she felt something soft beneath her shoes, an involuntary shudder made her close her eyes.

The flock lay huddled together, but some were still standing and stared dazedly at the light. The ram let out a long, tremulous bleat and took a few steps forward with an inquisitive air.

"What's the matter, King Herod?" asked the shepherd, stopping a moment to scratch between its horns. The ram delightedly lowered its head, and Mila admired those airy spirals.

"Are they really so fierce?" the woman asked.

"Sure they are...if you don't know how to handle them."

The shepherd sent his dog out of the shed, closed the gate, and climbed the stairs.

"It's cold!" exclaimed Mila, shivering and gazing up at the calm sky.

"What? The weather's been sweeter than a honeycomb, but after that oven, even a sneeze would catch cold."

"It was warm inside the shed."

"Very cozy. I'd rather have my tabernacle with four wisps of straw down there than the best bed with seven mattresses upstairs."

The kitchen had been transformed. A green tin

lantern, its panes gleaming like cut diamonds, cast sparkling cheer into every corner of the room. The tablecloth was in place beneath a soup tureen, and four yellow bowls shone like burnished gold. The shepherd put out his lamp and hung it beneath the mantelpiece.

"Well, let's start then, hermitess! You've fasted enough for one day I should think..." but he stopped in amazement.

"The tureen's empty! How can that be, Baldiret?"

The child, swallowing his laughter, smiled and rubbed his ear against his shoulder.

"Isn't there something you've forgotten? Your memory's terrible... We can't pour it straight from the pot; we'd scald our mustaches!"

And so saying, he went to the hearth, returned with the pot, and poured the soup into its tureen, from which a superb aroma rose, along with a spiraling billow of steam, making the tureen seem a vase of flowering tendrils. Everyone inhaled delightedly.

"What a wonderful smell!" cried Mila in surprise.

"Shepherd's soup, hermitess," replied Gaietà, returning the pot to its place. "A clove of garlic, a sprig of thyme, a few drops of oil, and let it all simmer. We men don't know how to fix fancy dishes like you do."

Despite these words, Mila, who found the soup exquisitely seasoned, felt her spirits revive with every spoonful, and when not one drop remained in her bowl, she gazed at the thin little man with eyes full of tearful gratitude: what luck to find such a good soul there! How could she have managed everything by herself that first night?

After the soup, Gaietà brought forth a pot of rice with cod-fish. Mila let out a chuckle: every grain was thick and split.

"Here's something to make you grow," announced the shepherd.

"I lost a whole night's sleep over this dish. I thought: 'What can I give them to chew on?' I couldn't think of anything good, and while I was puzzling over it, the sun came out. Then I leapt out of bed and, leaving the boy snoring, I headed down to the Nina, found Baldiret's mother, talked it over with her, and she set me straight."

He stopped to swallow a few forkfuls.

"Anyway, it hasn't turned out too badly. What do you think, hermitess, you who know about these things?"

Hunger can work miracles, and everyone thought the rice delicious even though it was overcooked.

The supper dispelled much of Mila's sadness. The hermitage no longer seemed so filthy, nor did the mountains' solitude appear so vast. That unknown shepherd lent the place a homey warmth, sweet and welcoming.

She went to bed with that impression, but the strange bed, lumpy and uneven, the very weight of her exhaustion, the muffled, constant sound of St. Pontius' Roar, which seeped into every nook and cranny of the room, and the belfry owl's screeches kept her awake for hours. Finally, in the early morning she drifted into a fitful sleep. She dreamt she was leaving the hermitage and returning home, but the more mountains she crossed, the more loomed up before her. Finally, after walking and walking, she saw a point of light in the distance. "Thank God," she thought. "It's the shepherd's lamp..." She excitedly started toward it, but as she drew near, she realized that the lights, of which there were now two, weren't the shepherd's lamp but St. Pontius' eyes: the same St. Pontius she had seen in the chapel. He was plowing around an olive tree, holding one hand on the plow while the other raised two stiff fingers, and he dragged that huge deformed foot that looked like Matias' tobacco pouch behind him. Mila tried to run, but the saint blocked her path and pelted her head with scarlet berries; and, feeling them drop into her mouth, she thought in terror that her skull must have split open. But no: they entered through the gash in her forehead, causing her such acute pain that she begged the saint for the love of God to stop. The saint, laughing so hard his fat lady's belly shook, sneeringly called out: "Hermitess, hermitess, hermitess!...," that name she so despised. Mila felt her heart breaking and burst into sobs; but the shepherd, stroking her like a child, dried her eyes and gently murmured: "Don't worry...we'll fix it."

III. Daylight

When Mila ventured onto the terrace outside the sitting room, her heart sank: the sun wasn't out! The iron railing oozed rusty liquid, which reddened her hands when she touched it. The flagstones in the courtyard were all wet, and drops of dew sparkled on the broken glass atop those blackened old walls around the hermitage.

The icy morning wind seemed full of tiny needles that pricked her skin.

Mila tried to get her bearings: on her left was the door to the kitchen. On her right, at the other end of the terrace and directly above the staircase, was another door she hadn't seen the night before. It was bolted.

"This house is full of bolts!" she thought.

She unbolted the door, opened it, and found herself on another broad terrace that faced due south. Matias had described this terrace to her, but she hadn't imagined it like that. It was bounded on the outside by a low wall filled with earth, from which masses of tangled leaves sprouted in green profusion. The bedrooms were on her left, and in each corner a battered tub encircled by iron bands held a rickety tree with dead twigs and just-opened buds. Matias had told her about that wonderful long terrace with its spectacular view, but it was merely another disappointment for Mila.

This terrace also seemed to sweat, like the iron railing around the other, and one might have thought the uneven walls caked with dark patches suffered from some hideous disease. The floor tiles reminded her of a neighbor in her parts whose teeth were so uneven that each went its separate way. Those tiles were just the same: cracked, sunken, gnawed like a cheese the rats had feasted on, covered with green patches of slimy moss that loosened the cement between them.

And the view? Mila looked from side to side. Everything was the same color: dull, ashy gray. Gray as that overcast, gloomy sky, gray as the mountain that rose to meet it, gray as the thick fog that hid everything but the upper half of the mountain: forms, distances, horizons...

Only by leaning over the railing could one see something different on the slopes around the hermitage: towering pines, just beginning to show new growth, clumps of kermes oak, an occasional tangle of blackberry bushes, and a few yards of ruined wall here, another fragment there, were the picture's sole additional ornaments.

Mila recalled her uneasiness about the hermitage. She remembered the past evening's vague impressions, her dream, and...she fled the terrace before her tears could begin to flow. At the door, she was surprised by a strange sound, a sort of prolonged mooing that seemed to come from below but also from the mountain... It had just sounded again. Baldiret was hanging over the side of the cistern, with his legs outside it, awakening all its indwelling echoes.

"Aaaah!" he cried as loudly as he could. "Aaaah!" replied all the sounds around him. And the boy, hanging head-down, wiggled his legs in delight.

Mila watched him anxiously, afraid he might fall in, but at that point the shepherd's voice rang out from the sheep shed.

"Hey, young fellow, you want a licking?" And the shepherd emerged to gently scold him: "Listen, little tweet-tweet, don't sing while people are asleep upstairs!"

"Not everyone, shepherd... Good morning!" said Mila, descending the steps.

"My God, is that you, hermitess? Good day to you! I figured you still had your head in the pillow. But I reckon you didn't sleep well if you're up and about so early..."

Mila guessed he had made her bed and had no wish to offend him.

"I wanted to see the house."

"Well, you won't have long to wait...and the hermit?"

"He was so tired he decided to sleep a little later."

"Fine, fine! You're a different sort from him. He always takes things easy, but you're the nervous type. Am I right?"

Mila smiled to hide her sadness that Matias' faults were so obvious.

"Bad business, those nerves," the shepherd continued. "They can ruin your peace of mind and addle your brain... I think your husband's got the right idea. Worries are like kites: the more string you give them, the higher they go... But here we are gabbing when I bet you want your breakfast. Let's go in."

"I'm not hungry."

"What? You're not fasting, are you? You've got to start the day with something, and I think the fire's gone out upstairs. Give me that bowl, boy. I'll get you some milk."

Mila tried to protest, but the shepherd ignored her.

"We already milked the nanny goat, so today it'll have to be sheep's milk." And seizing a ewe's hind legs, he started in with a will.

The milk squirted out in thin, straight jets like ivory needles, first from one teat and then another, while the bowl quickly filled with steamy white froth. When it was full, the shepherd rose, blew off the foam, and offered the milk to Mila, who shuddered in revulsion. The milk stank of sheep, and she could see others had drunk from that same bowl, but the shepherd offered it so kindly that she dared not refuse. Mila took the bowl and emptied it, holding her breath all the while and making a great effort not to screw up her face.

"Well done! You'll soon put some meat on those bones! Now, since the hermit's asleep, let's get cracking around the house."

"Don't you have to take the flock out today?"

The shepherd laughed. "It's too early! I'll wait till the dew dries. This isn't the plain, which starts to bake first thing in the morning. We won't see the sun till ten o'clock."

"You mean it'll come out at ten?"

"That's what I reckon. I don't mean we'll get burned, but a few rays will peek through..." And looking up, he added: "Those clouds are thin."

"Oh, if only it would shine just a little!" exclaimed Mila, clasping her hands. "Everything would seem different. I got so sad watching that fog from the terrace."

The shepherd laughed louder.

"God Almighty! If the fog bothers you, you sure can't be from around here. You see, I like the fog; it sets me thinking... I like to pasture my sheep up there in the sun and look down on the clouds below... On some paths I hear deep voices but you can't see a soul, so I guess the fairies must be admiring themselves in some pool while they do their laundry... The fog's pretty, don't you think, hermitess?"

As he talked, the shepherd climbed the steps to the kitchen, where he made a fire while Mila threw out what was left of the soup and hung the pot on its hook. Then they went out again, unbolted and unlocked the gate, and clambered after the boy and dog, who ran gleefully ahead, whistling and barking.

The hermitage stood on a slope that led down to St.

Pontius' Pass. On the right, at some distance, you could see the pine groves that covered Roquís Gros, and on the left Roquís Mitjà reared its bald head. Along the slope were patches of terraced land, with a few olive trees near the bottom and closer by, some almond trees clothed in exuberant greenery, as if still rejoicing in their recent flowering.

About five feet from the hermitage stood the crumbling walls of a sheep fold, with two old wells and big puddles of rainwater close by, and behind the fold, the slope was adorned by clumps of rockrose and flowering rosemary, among which two fig trees like skeletal coral growths sent forth a thousand twisted, mottled branches. Beyond everything, between the two Roquissos, a smooth, squat mountain rose like a hump from its long, stony backbone.

They descended the steps that led to the terraces, at whose entrance two ancient cypresses leaned against each other like a couple of drunken giants, mingling their green tunics clawed by the nails of time.

"Look, hermitess, that land is ripe for planting... I spent my spare time plowing it, so the hermit can grow whatever he likes. If you could have seen these almond trees a few weeks ago, you'd have loved them... They looked like the French mountains in winter, all white... See all those leaves?"

But Mila was staring at a hill in the distance.

"What's that strange thing, shepherd?"

"The Elephant. People around here call it the Husk, but I like the other name better. Better likeness, y'know?" And hearing Mila confess that she didn't know what an elephant was, the shepherd explained.

"Biggest animals on earth, I reckon: each leg as thick as a tree trunk, with heavy wrinkled skin. But the strangest part is they have two tails: one like other beasts and a big one hanging from their heads."

Mila looked at the shepherd. He was serious; he wasn't making fun of her. Surprised, she wondered if he was as fond of tall tales as Matias, and her admiration for him weakened.

"I saw some once on the road to Murons, with a crowd of people who put on shows in the villages. At first I was scared, y'know, but afterwards I wished I had one... Mighty beasts, by God! That's the only time I ever saw them, and God knows how many years ago it was. I was still a bachelor."

Mila stopped, surprised.

"Are you married, shepherd?"

"Widowed, hermitess."

They picked their way along slippery gullies, and he took her hand lest she fall. Then he calmly began to talk: "I'd just arrived in these parts and was working at St. Pontius' Farm, where I spied a servant girl pretty as a flower. I watched her week after week, till finally I got her alone and said: 'Lluci, I need a wife... Couldn't you use a husband?' So without more fuss we started courting. Seems like she'd been thinking the same thing for a while. And we got married... She was kin to the lady of the house, and since I always gave them an honest day's work, they asked us to stay on till we were ready to settle down, so we stayed. They're good folks down there at St. Pontius, hermitess! When hard times come, they're kind... That's why I'm still friends with them, just like they were family."

"And what about your wife, shepherd?" asked Mila, seeing that the topic pleased the little man.

"She only lasted eight months, hermitess! Poor girl, she was good as gold!"

The shepherd paused awhile and then continued: "One day she'd swept the courtyard. The wagon was standing loaded at the entrance, about to leave, but just as she went through the gate, the horse reared up and trapped her between the gate and the wheel."

"Holy Virgin!"

"They say she screamed and tried to dodge."

The shepherd lowered his head and then added uncertainly: "Everyone came running, but since I was a long way away, they sent someone to fetch the doctor and a boy to look for me. The doctor got there first... When I arrived, I heard the cries, like an animal having its throat cut... It was horrible... And upstairs they showed me a little angel you could have held in the palm of your hand... God help us!"

Mila gazed pityingly at the man, whose lips were pursed and whose eyes were red.

To say something, she asked: "And you never remarried?"

The shepherd blinked and hesitated: "I never had the heart, hermitess! I always hear those cries and see that little angel... God sees everything and we're nothing but dust...but after all that!"

And the shepherd scratched his head, as if still struggling to accept the news.

Mila looked at him differently now. That friendly soul had also been stung by grief's viper, and after all those years the wound had yet to heal.

But even so, he didn't spend his days crying and complaining. He bravely took life as it came and tried to help others. He wasn't like Matias, not at all. If he said he'd seen an elephant, well, then he'd seen one.

They left the hermitage behind, making their way over crags and along narrow gullies.

Roquís Gros seemed to hover above their heads, and the far-off rumble Mila had heard all night grew rapidly louder, drowning out the boy's laughter and the dog's barks, which rang out sometimes ahead and sometimes behind them.

"Where are we going, shepherd?" asked the woman.

"To the Roar, hermitess. I heard you two talking about it, and I want you to see it. The water does you a world of good, much better than at the hermitage. I was lucky when that tragedy happened. I got so downhearted that the doctor in Murons began to worry, but then St. Pontius pulled me out of it all by himself... A blessed saint, St. Pontius, hermitess..."

Mila again recalled her dream and that grotesque saint, with one hand on the plow and throwing berries at her forehead with the other. She shuddered and unconsciously touched the gash.

"It'll get better by itself, hermitess. It's already closed up, and soon you won't even know where it was." The path twisted and turned around boulders, some of which had fallen in avalanches, and the noise from the Roar bounced from one to another like a captive beast straining against its cage.

Mila was making her way down a steep slope when she heard the shepherd's dog Mussol bounding toward her. She quickly threw her arms around a boulder just as the dog sped past like a bullet, brushing against her skirt. Baldiret saw it all from above and burst out laughing.

Mila turned around, raised her head, and looked up at that ruddy face with its big green eyes. The boy blushed and stopped laughing, while Mila felt a feverish glow in her belly. Seeing her there, the shepherd called up from below, and Mila quickly finished her descent.

Suddenly it seemed that the mountain had swallowed them or that they had entered another chapel. Darkness, damp, and chill filled the grotto, at whose end there was a hole: the mouth of a stream that issued mysteriously from the mountain's uncharted depths. From that stream gushed a jet of molten silver which fell, with billows of spray, into a large stone basin it had hollowed out and then poured bubbling into a twisting brook, seeking the larger current that would bear it down to the plain.

"What clear water!" Mila exclaimed.

"None better, hermitess," replied the shepherd enthusiastically. "We should have brought some jugs, but I'd better warn you: never drink from that basin... Sick people and animals bathe there, and even though the Roar cleans it every day, it can hurt your eyes."

"What's the basin, shepherd?"

"That big pool there... You see how it's hollowed out? That's why I made a little channel to drink from. When you want to fill your jug, put the mouth here..."

As if to show what the shepherd meant, Baldiret put his own mouth to the little channel and took some big gulps.

"Won't that make him sick after the milk?" asked Mila.

"I never heard of the Roar hurting anyone, hermitess. It only cures people. You see, St. Pontius knows what he's up to. Study the letters on those paintings in the chapel and you'll learn all about his miracles. It's quite a story, I can tell you!"

The boy, whose faun-like face was still dripping, had stepped back from the Roar. Mila stared at him dazedly, still feeling that glow in her belly.

"Miracles, miracles!" the shepherd said. "Go ahead!" Bending over and saying a silent prayer, she bravely drank the icy water, which made her teeth ache and took her breath away.

On their way back, Mussol's barks were answered, as they had been the night before, by the echoing mountains.

Mila smiled and said: "Last night that sound gave me a start!"

"Don't you know what it is?"

"Matias said something about fairies...but what are they?"

"Ladies who cast spells! I can see the hermit didn't

explain much to you. I'll tell you a story later about why they mock everything they hear..."

Baldiret, who had been walking ahead of them, caught the shepherd's words, let them overtake him, and seized the man's hand.

Gaietà laughed.

"Look at him. As soon as he hears the word *story*, he'll stick to you like a leech. He'd sell his soul for a fairytale, wouldn't you?"

The boy rubbed his ear against his shoulder, smiled, and clung to the shepherd's hand.

"But the story about the Old Man is too long, and we've got to make lunch. Let's leave it for another day."

Baldiret gloomily hung his head.

The shepherd burst out laughing.

"Don't be so glum, my friend! I'll tell you while the hermitess cooks lunch. That'll do, won't it?"

The child's face brightened, and, releasing the shepherd's hand, he dashed after Mussol.

"Hey, watch where you're going! Those buckthorns'll give you a nose like a Jew!" the man shouted, seeing the boy chasing the dog, and he tenderly added: "He's off like a bat out of hell... One day he'll fall off a cliff, God preserve us!... Ah, it's wonderful to be young!"

"Isn't he from St. Pontius' Farm?" Mila asked.

"Yes, hermitess. He's the lady's son. I love him because he's so sweet-natured, just like a lamb. When I get lonely up here, I always send for him. He'd never leave me, and it's all because of those fairy tales, y'know?... In the winter, when I'm shut up in his house, he makes me rack my brains for new ones..."

They reached the slope behind the hermitage, and the shepherd raised his head.

"What did I tell you, hermitess? Look how the sun's shining!"

And in fact, between the Elephant and Highpeak a

pale shaft of light, like a faded luminous flower, shot its feeble rays across the icy gray sky.

As they entered the hermitage, sheep and lambs began bleating, Baldiret sang like a sparrow, all the doors were thrown open and the house filled with life. But Mila's heart sank: Matias was still sleeping like a baby, with all his cares tucked beneath the pillow.

While the shepherd watched the soup, she went to wake her husband.

"Aren't you ashamed? It's lunchtime..."

But then she heard the shepherd in the sitting room.

"Now that I think of it, hermitess... Would you like to see the belfry before lunch?"

"Just as you like, shepherd."

The staircase was narrow, and its rickety planks had been gnawed by termites. From time to time, a slender window admitted a crack of light. Peering through those slits, as through a stereopticon at a fair, Mila saw fragmented pictures solely composed of sky and mountain, mountain and sky.

They reached the belfry, which was shaped like a candle snuffer. Mila looked up with a twinge of fear at the bells' great black mouths, whose hard, circular lips enclosed those clappers hanging like tongues. But they didn't hang idly. As soon as the shepherd grasped the rope, they burst into wild cries that echoed through the surrounding countryside.

"What are you doing, shepherd?" asked Mila, covering her ears.

"I'm celebrating your arrival, hermitess! I had to do something to welcome you; otherwise, no one would know we have new guests..." and laughing gaily, he went on, but upon seeing that he was deafening her, he dropped the rope.

"Your ears better get used to that song, 'cause on the saint's day everyone in these hills will have to hear it."

The fragments seen through the slits had now broadened into a whole panorama, devoid of anything but endless sky and mountain, mountain and sky.

On one side they saw Roquís Gros, on the other rose Roquís Mitjà's long whale-like back, and before them a vast slope covered with puddles and scrub, beyond which other distant mountains rose, still half-shrouded in fog.

The woman stood there, gazing out with wide eyes and clenched teeth, feeling a strange trembling within her.

The shepherd noticed her mood and said: "When the sun comes out you'll see something beautiful, hermitess. Everything sparkles like rock salt or cut glass. It looks like the mountains down there are lit from underneath, and the Roquís stares down at them, green with envy. Over that hill is Murons, a big town, and further on you come to Badblood Creek, where the water's always red..."

The shepherd interrupted himself: "You know why it's red?"

Mila had no idea.

"That hermit should have his ears boxed for not telling you a thing or two about these hills... That's why you can't see how pretty it all is. You have to hear about past fairs to look forward to the next one. And besides, you should know there was a town on the other side of the Roquís where a Moorish king had a mighty castle. He ruled these mountains and wouldn't let anyone pass through except girls from fifteen to twenty years old that his men would carry off to the castle. If he liked them he kept them; but if he didn't, off with their heads, which he tossed into Badblood Creek...that's how it got its name and why the water's so red. And every Christmas if you stand at midnight on the Pont del Cop that crosses those waters, you'll hear a wailing and a moaning that'll make your hair stand on end."

Mila shivered.

"And why is that, shepherd?"

"It's the heads of those dead lasses he didn't want, bumping against the bridge and lamenting..."

The woman paled at that grisly tale, but the shepherd's cheerful face calmed her, seeming to say all was not dreadful and tragic in those dark mountains. He went on, laughing: "Why do you keep looking up like a blind man? You should look all around... What do you think of that down there?"

She turned to look down.

A great yard stretched before her, surrounded by walls and cypresses even mightier than on the terraces, but straight and bushy, their trunks white with age and thick as massive columns. Some stone steps led to a pine grove below. As Mila admired that severe and majestic sight, she noticed a blue spot making its way among the green trees. Her sharp eyes quickly identified it.

"That's a man, shepherd!" she cried in amazement, as if rediscovering something she thought never to see again.

The shepherd frowned.

"Anima," he said, and turning to her he gravely added: "Watch out for him, hermitess... He's the nastiest character in these mountains."

The pale sun had burnt the last wisps of fog from Roquís Mitjà, whose bald crest was bathed in gold.

IV. Housecleaning

Mila spent two weeks in a state of female intoxication: she was cleaning. With all the doors and windows flung open, her skirts hiked up and her hair dishevelled, she didn't stop from sunrise to sundown.

She had found everything like a pigsty. The walls, which hadn't been whitewashed for many years, were covered with fingerprints, names, and obscene drawings left by visitors on the saint's day. Spiders, masters of all they surveyed, dangled from the ceilings and had filled every corner with their webs. There was such a thick layer of grime on the floors that one couldn't tell what they were made of, and the woodwork cried out for a carpenter's plane.

Every room in the house had to be scrubbed, but the dirtiest of all were the kitchen above and the chapel below. The kitchen concerned her most, since she'd have to spend the most time there, but who could possibly scour those smoke-blackened walls and ceiling? What arms had strength to scrape that solid filth off the sink? Who could polish all those brass and copper pots that hung, green and fly-specked beneath their coat of dust?

Seeing her so discouraged, the shepherd tried to comfort her: "You know, this hermitage is like Heaven, but Heaven wouldn't be Heaven if the people there didn't keep it clean. The hermitess before you was the biggest slut alive. In the ten years she was here she never touched a broom... The pigs she kept always had plenty of company, and the hens would peck at your plate while you were eating. I'm amazed I didn't get sick during the summers...it must be my constitution... I even told the *senyor* rector at confession how filthy everything was, and he gave her a talking to, but he was wasting his breath. People can't just change overnight. The only solution was to throw them out... Houses don't turn into homes all by themselves, and that hermitess wasn't woman enough to tackle this one, but you shouldn't lose heart so quickly! A little touch here and there, and everything'll shine like new..."

Mila closed her eyes and plunged in like a swimmer diving into the sea. Matias, hoping to postpone the monumental house-cleaning that troubled his lazy soul, invited her to Murons and a couple of dozen other places, but she flatly refused.

"As long as this house is a dung heap, don't talk to me about sightseeing. Go and see the rector yourself and get us supplies."

So Matias was forced to act as quartermaster till everything was in order. After all, he preferred that to constantly fetching water from the well and answering the questions she pestered him with whenever he came into view. Having done the kitchen, Mila decided to work systematically from the easiest to the hardest task and from top to bottom, but she didn't enter the chapel till everything else was so spick and span that the shepherd said it looked like angels had licked it clean.

When her broom and feather dusters stormed the chapel, it seemed the very mountains trembled. Saints swayed on their altars, terrified rats scurried to and fro, hunks of molding fell to earth, wax arms and legs were snapped in two... And amid the tumult and thick clouds of dust, you could see Mila ardently wheeling, attacking here and there, sparing no hole or corner. She abandoned herself to that onslaught, feeling a voluptuous thrill in her revolutionary ardor.

And one afternoon, when she had climbed onto a ledge above the altar and was polishing a candleholder shaped like an angel, she suddenly noticed that the light had dimmed and, turning around, spied a man in the doorway.

She quickly and a little confusedly climbed down, trying to keep him from seeing her legs. She was flushed and agitated, her candid eyes shone beneath their dust-whitened lashes, and the red kerchief around her head made her look like a mischievous boy caught in some prank.

The visitor stood there staring, as though surprised.

He was a barefoot middle-aged peasant, misshapen, dressed in a crumpled blue jacket and some torn yellow corduroy trousers held up by a rope. The man was shirtless, and beneath a beat-up old stocking cap, a bony greenish ridge protruded, holding two tiny deep-set eyes of indeterminate color that stirred uneasily like insects in the grass.

"Good afternoon," Mila said.

He remained silent, glowering at her from beneath those brows.

Mila felt herself blushing and smiled awkwardly. Then the man seemed to rouse himself and burst into laughter.

"*Hoo hoo hoo...* good afternoon."

His voice was hoarse, and as he laughed that strange laugh, he closed his eyes and bared his teeth, which were white as pearls, while his upper gums were brown as chocolate.

The man stuck his hand down his trousers and scratched his belly, as if uncertain what to do next. Suddenly he muttered, in a singsong voice, that after coming down from Cockfoot, near Highpeak, he was thirsty and had entered the chapel to ask for a drink of water.

"All right," the woman cheerfully replied. "Please

come up!" And after mounting the steps to the bedroom, she led him through the house to the kitchen.

Mila offered him a chair and a wineskin, but the man preferred to remain standing. His sole wish was to drink, which he did at great length... His throat gurgled rhythmically like a bottle being emptied, while his huge, pointed Adam's apple bobbed up and down. Then he breathed heavily, and, being covered with sweat, he lifted his cap to wipe his brow.

Mila saw the strangest forehead she'd ever beheld, a forehead that scarcely seemed human: long and pear-shaped, as if the top and sides had been pressed in a vice, and with such prominent brows that they resembled an arching cornice: the bony greenish ridge that protruded beneath his cap.

The man explained that he'd risen before sunrise to seek out rabbit holes for his ferret the next day, and that the week before he'd caught six of them in one morning and he reckoned he'd soon catch as many again. He sold them to hotels and gentlemen in Murons, and ferrets were hotter on a trail than any hunter alive.

He was unused to conversation, and as he talked, his glance wandered evasively, while his hoarse voice some-times grew muffled, as though he'd stepped behind a curtain.

Once the man had gone out through the courtyard, Mila crossed the sheep shed and storeroom on her way back to the chapel.

The sun poured through the open door, striking the flagstones and presbytery steps, glittering in reflective patches on all the walls.

As Mila climbed onto the altar to scrub a wooden angel's hand and thigh, a thought tormented her: "Where have I seen that man before? I'm sure I've seen him somewhere. I remember those strange gums and white teeth..."

But since her lazy memory refused to aid her, after puzzling awhile she stopped worrying and, eager to attack the saint and those offerings left before him, she forgot all about her guest.

Mila lived in terror of that ill-sculpted saint's wicked glance. His lower lids sagged like those of certain old people, revealing red circles around such uneven eyes that the whole face seemed twisted into a grimace. That crooked visage, that bulging paunch, and that huge, pouch-like foot recalled her dream of the saint's cruel bullying.

And the offerings, those decrepit little arms and legs that looked like they'd been chopped off dead children, those canes smudged with the dirt of sweaty hands, those heads of hair, that forest of painted boards nailed to the walls and columns, seemed, like some cynical cripple, to threaten all the ills they depicted. And so, as soon as her fingertips lighted upon one of those dusty relics, a violent shudder ran through her and she snatched her hand away, postponing that unpleasant task, always postponing it, as though hoping someone would come to her aid.

And she went back to polishing altars, scrubbing flagstones, and rearranging candles: that flock of candles in all sizes, some as thick as arms or thighs, and all wound round with chains of flowers and gilded letters on brightly colored strips of paper...

But when the peeled, faded gilding sparkled as best it could and the saints, scrubbed as though they were on their way to church, smiled their saintly smiles from their perches, and all the altar-cloths had been mended and the white, aromatic tapers arranged around the presbytery, since the desired assistance had still not materialized, Mila was forced to decide what to do about all those offerings, which hung like bizarre stalagtites in a forgotten cavern.

"Help me, Matias! There's so much to do, I'll never

finish!" she had begged her husband, her eyes full of terror. But Matias just scratched the back of his neck and mumbled that on that very day the rector had summoned him.

Mila's frozen smile cut short his explanations.

"Go ahead, then, go see him. He must get lonely without you."

And in a blaze of fury, she drew a bucket of water from the well, picked up her soap and scrub brushes, and stormed into the chapel. All alone, and with such speed that her hands seemed to multiply, she set to work. First she took down the votive boards and dusted, scrubbed and rinsed them till they looked brand new. She was reassured and surprised to see an unknown world revive beneath her brush: a world of brilliant colors, objects and scenes she recognized, of mountains whose sharp, symmetrical ridges were outlined against the sky, of women tumbling down stairs, their hair streaming behind them, of red horses frolicking in emerald meadows, of houses devoured by flames, of shipwrecked vessels with crews on deck, their arms raised heavenward like "y's" in a grade school primer... a bright chaos of violent tones, the products of vivid and expressive imaginations, childlike and primitive, that exhaled a kind of secret charm, the perfume of a savage faith that gradually invaded Mila, soothing her fears and rousing her curiosity, along with flashes of sympathy and instants of terror that passed and left her calm. From then on, the boards became familiar objects, and when they all shone like new and she laid them in the sun to dry, they even made her laugh. She compared herself to the Old Storyteller, a tall, gaunt man who every year visited her village fair and set up his stand in the square in front of the blacksmith's shop, from whose walls he hung folded pieces of paper on a long string. Those papers, at which she had stared in wonder as a child, also depicted fires, falls, people dragged behind horses...calamities of all kinds, and legends even more dreadful than the calamities. The same as those votive offerings, the only difference being that the former were called *disasters* and the latter *miracles*, and while there were no saints in the former, every votive picture included St. Pontius, surrounded by a circle of clouds, with one hand raised and the other on his crozier.

That universal devotion to the saint was what Mila couldn't understand, though she saw it all around her. Often, by reverently raising her eyes to gaze upon him and through a great effort of will, she could achieve an attitude of respectful veneration, but some unconscious skepticism always renewed her doubts, making her sense some incompatibility, like a secret feud, between her and the mountains' glorious patron.

And to dispel that impression, which despite herself she found disturbing, she returned to her work with renewed vigor.

After the painted boards, it was time to clean the ostrich eggs, brought from the other side of the world and suspended on thick silk cords, and those model ships as covered with pulleys and rigging as full-sized vessels, the heads of hair, rough and crackly like armfuls of wheat, which, though long dead, still seemed to reek of sickroom sweat, the misshapen, hoof-like footwear that had shod deformed feet, rosaries from Jerusalem with beads the size of big almonds, and...such a jumble of odds and ends that the chapel looked like a bazaar.

Among all those objects that meant nothing to Mila, she found one that touched her heart. It was a little dress trimmed with delicate lace. The silk had yellowed, the lace was unraveling, and the humidity in that chapel, closed for many years, had turned the dust to hard gum and made the fabric rigid. Mila tried to clean it but found the folds stuck together. The dress was full of holes, as if someone had taken in ice pick to it, and the fear that it would crumble like a lump of sugar made her leave it alone. But every time she saw it hanging stiffly from the wall, she imagined the soft flesh, anxiously clenched fists, big staring eyes and pouting lips of some girl a few months old. She had always, even before her marriage, been touched by such trifles.

Finally, when she'd cleaned everything, including the votive offerings, and was cheerfully scouring the last basin among the cypresses, she spied the shepherd's woolen cap. He was descending Roquís Mitjà, followed by his flock and Baldiret. The man walked slowly, carrying a stout crook under his arm.

Without knowing why, Mila felt a sudden urge to seize his attention and began singing "The Merchant's Daughter" loudly enough so he could hear her. Gaietà raised his head and looked down.

Mila then, also without knowing why, regretted what she had done.

The shepherd let the boy and his flock continue toward the sheep shed, while he approached Mila.

"Good afternoon. I see you're still at it, hermitess. Don't you think you're overdoing things a little? The poor saints aren't used to so much fuss, and I bet they don't like it either... Heed my words and take things easier. If you tackle everything straight off you'll have nothing left to work at!"

The shepherd laughed, standing beneath a cypress with his legs spread apart.

Mila, who felt happier than a lark, carefully showed him everything she had done.

He praised it all with simple words that sounded like courtly gallantries.

"Well, hermitess, I must say St. Pontius never had it so good! Everything shines like gold in the noonday sun. As soon as I laid eyes on you, I figured we were in luck...

First thing tomorrow morning, I'll go to Murons and tell the *senyor* rector to come and look. I'm sure he'll sing your praises."

"Oh no, shepherd!" cried Mila. "Don't let him come till the cloths are all washed and ironed; otherwise it won't look right."

"Well then, let's wait till they're ready, if you promise it won't take long... because I'm eager for him to see it, y'know?" And he suddenly added: "Did you clean all the miracles?"

"That's what I've been up to these past three days, shepherd!"

And with a mischievous gleam in her eye, she added: "As far as I can see, St. Pontius did a few too many!"

"That's heathen talk and the Devil's words! You're a bit of a heretic, aren't you?" asked the shepherd, half-joking and half-serious.

"Who, me?"

"I've seen you giving that poor saint dirty looks!" Gaietà stopped laughing and said: "But it's badly done, hermitess. You should love St. Pontius. If you knew how he helps people in distress. You just kneel before him, tell him your troubles, and the next thing you know it seems like those eyes are staring straight at you and all your worries disappear. Oh, that St. Pontius!"

And the shepherd shook his head, looking thoughtful and deeply moved.

Mila felt that he had left her and withdrawn into another world.

But he soon returned, with his smile and that twinkle in his eye.

"You know what I'm thinking now, hermitess? We'll have to go through the place inch by inch, and you can show me what you've done." And since she looked at him questioningly, he added: "Let me find the boy and lock up my sheep. I'll be back in a jiffy."

And he strode off toward the hermitage.

"What a good man! He acts like everyone's father or brother!" thought Mila, seeing first his legs and then his cap disappear behind the hill. And once he was out of sight, she bent to pick up the half-scrubbed basin.

It was an old brass basin, around which long letters had been engraved, but they were in Latin and she couldn't read them. A blow to the rim had left a dent the size of a hazelnut, and Mila had needed her nails and the juice of a lemon to get the tarnish out of it, but now she could see her face reflected in the bottom, tiny but bright and detailed as a tinted photo.

"How pretty I look there!" she thought, and impulsively bringing the basin to her lips, she kissed her own reflection.

She blushed and looked cautiously about her.

"Heavens! I wonder what's got into me today!" she thought confusedly, feeling her eyes fill with tears. And when the shepherd returned, she smiled shyly, like a child who has broken something.

The shepherd excitedly brandished a thick reed and asked her for a bit of candle. He then cut open one end of the reed, inserted the tallow stub, and led her into the chapel.

"Could you shut the doors please, hermitess?"

Mila went toward the chapel doors and pulled them partly shut, but she was struck by the setting sun, which poured through the crack and hung blood-red on the crest of the furthest mountain.

"How strange, the sun...looks like it's dying... It's sad to have to die..." And like a flash, the idea of death shot through her turbulent, unconscious spirit, making her blood run cold.

When she turned around, she couldn't keep from crying out in amazement. All the torches and candles in the chapel were lit. Amid a sea of sparkling gold, the little flames flickered in the darkness as if the shrine were a magic carpet shaken by concealed hands.

The shepherd stood in the middle of the chapel, holding his reed and looking about him.

"Mother of God! Why did you do that?"

The shepherd slowly approached her.

"The people in these parts are stupid and don't do things right. They bring the saint candles and then leave him in the dark all year. They don't even light them on the morning of his day, and as soon as the service is over he's back in the dark again...and besides, not a soul really worships him like he deserves... All they care about is eating, dancing, and making fools of themselves...it's sad to see... You know, a party for everyone's a party for no one. I'd rather celebrate by myself... That way no one can disturb me."

He touched her arm and led her to the end of the chapel, to its darkest nook beneath the choir loft, and made her sit down beside him on the stone floor.

"Take a good look, hermitess... It's not this bright outside even at midday, but the idiots around here wouldn't get the point. If you only knew how sorry I feel for them sometimes! Poor things! They live and die without having any fun... "

He fell silent. Out of the corner of her eye, Mila saw him sitting immobile, as if dazzled, gazing at the sea of lights; and she, in that dark corner, felt his warm body against her right arm, looked at his beardless face in the candlelight, his head full of daydreams, and understood once again that he was far, far away...wandering through distant and mysterious landscapes.

And then the indifference that had always enclosed her like a long, blank wall, began to crack, while troubling new sensations, secret mountain sprites, began slowly to filter through the crevices.

Late one afternoon, * as Mila was brushing a head of hair – long, thick, falling straight as a waterfall – she saw the shepherd leading his flock and Baldiret down to the hermitage.

They reached her just as, after bidding them good afternoon, she was starting back to the chapel, where she would return the hair to its place. But the shepherd caught her arm with his crook and halted her.

"Hermitess, do you know what you've got in your hands?"

"No...what is it?"

"Everyone around here knows... By God, it's a lovely story."

"Is it? Then please tell me," begged Mila, whose curiosity had been aroused.

"It won't take long, hermitess..." and turning to Baldiret, Gaietà smiled playfully and said: "Take these sheep in while I tell her..."

"Hey!" cried the boy, glancing at him disappointedly.

"Have you hurt yourself?" asked the shepherd, winking at Mila.

"No," replied the lad, surprised at the question.

"When I heard you shout..." And seeing him blush, Gaietà added: "Don't worry, I can see you want to hear the story too. God help us, I wouldn't want you to feel unhappy... Anyway, a rest won't hurt before the sun goes down...and the sheep won't mind, will they? They've already had their nap on Highpeak."

And seating himself on a low wall that encircled the yard, while his flock scattered, munching the grass between the steps and flagstones, he began to speak to the child and woman, whose eyes never left him.

_____

*Here begins the only fragment conserved of the two unpublished chapters referred to in the author's *Foreword*.

"Hermitess, that's not just any old head of hair... You should know that many years ago, there was a noble lady with such pretty locks that everyone in Murons called her sunshine: *Sol*. When she pinned up those locks, they glittered brighter than any jewel. By the time she was sixteen, she had more suitors than there were folds in her skirts, and you know, skirts were broad in the old days...no one used to worry about saving cloth, though now they're narrower than a choirboy's surplice... Anyway, getting back to the young lady, at sixteen she had more suitors than stars in the sky. And they came in all shapes and sizes: high class and down-to-earth, rich and humble, handsome and plain, so old they could hardly walk straight and so young that if you squeezed their chops, mother's milk would squirt out. There wasn't a bachelor or widower within a hundred miles of Murons who wasn't dying to marry her. But she spurned them all, one after the other, no matter what they offered or how often they bribed her maid. Till finally a rumor started that she was so proud of her beauty she wouldn't give it to anyone but a genuine prince. And as that rumor spread, all those jilted suitors started talking about how stuck up she was. They made fun of the lady, but it wasn't what they thought, you see, because she didn't turn them down out of pride but because she and her cousin were in love and she'd promised to be his wife. Unfortunately, that cousin was poorer than a church-mouse and her parents wanted her to marry someone with a crest above his door, a carriage, and a carpeted parlor. You see, old people aren't as flighty as young ones and know that two and two makes four. So the cousin sailed for America, where he hoped to make his fortune, and from then on she waited patiently, sure he'd come back and make her happy..."

"And did he?" asked Mila, her eyes as big as saucers.

"He did indeed, hermitess! She was a good catch, that

Sol! But you can't collect doubloons like snails on a rainy evening. The cousin took no less than twenty years to fill his pockets. So when he finally came back and spied the lady, who was almost forty, she wasn't nearly as fresh and pretty as when he'd first laid eyes on her.

"He was disappointed, but since his cousin still had those beautiful tresses, that made up for a lot. By now people were talking about their wedding day, but the Devil, who's always on the lookout, afflicted him with such a terrible chill that they had to call in the doctors and healers. And after examining him, they said what he'd caught was so dreadful that he was at death's door and only a miracle could save him. Imagine how pale the lady turned when she heard that news! And since she didn't want to die an old maid after putting off her marriage, she knelt before St. Pontius, whom she'd always worshipped, and prayed for a miracle. But the cousin went from bad to worse and no miracle happened. Then the lady clasped her hands and, gazing toward Heaven, told the saint that if he saved her beloved she'd give him her most prized possession. And when the saint saw what a fix she was in, he took pity on her and gave her to understand that she shouldn't worry, he'd straighten everything out.

"And in fact, thanks to his intercession, everything did work out. The very next day her cousin began to mend. Seeing how her prayers had been answered, the lady took up her hoop and embroidered a fine ribbon. She finished just before the sick man left his bed. The next morning, without breathing a word to anyone, she took some shears and started up the mountain. She felt weak as she climbed, and when she made the first cut she almost fainted, but she'd made a promise and had to keep it if she didn't want to roast in Hell. You can't haggle with a saint, so after thinking it over, she picked up the shears again and snip...snip...snip...she cut off every last hair.

Then she tied that embroidered ribbon around her tresses and hung them in the chapel. When she came down the mountain she wasn't the same woman, and when her cousin saw that cropped head, which made her look like a galley slave, he stepped back and began to cross himself like he'd seen a ghost. He paled and nearly got sick again. He tried to steel himself for a while, but one day he slipped away and went back to America. When he got there, he sent a letter telling her he'd arrived safe and sound, thank God, but business wasn't good and he'd have to stay forever, and that after thinking over the marriage, he'd decided that after so many years, they'd better let it drop. When the lady heard this, she swooned like she'd been struck by lightning, and a month later she entered St. Clara's convent as a novice... And like I said, ever since, her hair's been hanging in your chapel, where no moth or anything else has ever touched it. When I got here, it still glittered like gold, and the old hermitess used to wash and brush it once a year so it would stay beautiful. But the last one, like I told you a thousand times, had no business being here and never cleaned it, which is how it got so faded, you see?"

That pathetic story touched Mila's heart and inspired her to imitate the previous hermitess, for after all, that relic of the lovelorn lady, which at first had disgusted her, was as deserving as anything else in the chapel. Instead of hanging it back up, therefore, the next morning she took it to the courtyard where she would be undisturbed and slowly untied the ribbon, whose faded silk, brittle as a piece of old paper, crackled and split at the slightest contact. She stayed out in the sun till midday, soaping and rinsing that immense head of hair, which gently swayed in the basin of water like a school of undulating eels. Her heart swelled to see the compact mass grow a little each time she rubbed it, spreading beneath her hands' knowing caresses, losing its dull appearance, and recovering its former luster and suppleness. Once it was clean, she worked a few drops of oil into it, hung it up to dry, and went in to lunch. Upon her return to the sunlit yard, she was astonished at the spectacle that greeted her: the dried tresses sparkled like a jewel... The shepherd's words had been true! Then she understood why the lady's nickname had been Sol, and Mila grasped the magnitude of her sacrifice. For certainly those fair locks had been unequalled in their time. Mila gazed upon them, overwhelmed by waves of joy, her nostrils trembling and her mouth slightly open, and then plunged her hands into the splendid skein, rubbing it voluptuously against her skin, burying her face in it, winding it round her arms like a warm snake... Suddenly, raising her head with female pride and drying her eyes, she muttered tensely: "I wouldn't give up something like that for all the men on earth."

V. Counting Days

Mila, who had nearly completed her monumental cleaning, no longer felt like such a stranger in the hermitage. One might have scrutinized it inch by inch without finding a speck of dust or a neglected cranny. That jumble of useless objects piled behind the altar was now stored in the chapel basement, and the shepherd had scoured the nearby fields for straw, which he dried in the sun and Mila strewed about the sheep shed. Even the drainpipe beneath the sink had been unclogged with buckets of water, and the rickety steps in the belltower had been nailed firmly in place. Matias' shiftlessness obliged Mila to travel often to Murons, for her husband never brought home anything useful, but gradually she stocked the larder — now with an eight-pound sack of flour, now with another of potatoes, now with some dried cod — while she adorned the hood over the fireplace with a thick band of green paper and the shelf for the pots with a few white plates and a half-dozen cups. In the yard outside the sheep shed, some new rabbits wrinkled their noses ironically, and in the shadowy depths of that same shed, two hens sat roosting. She had planted a vegetable garden on one of the terraces, and finally, in a brigade of cracked pots and basins, red carnations opened their fiery eyes, burst forth in double miracles, and shamelessly offered their cheeks to the sun's kisses.

Mila owed those jeweled plants, her house's gayest note, to the shepherd's thoughtfulness. One day she had told him she preferred flowers to vegetables, and the next morning he made her follow him to St. Pontius' Farm, where he asked the lady, whose name was Marieta, for a few cuttings. But Marieta, who was generous by nature and whose garden was in full bloom, told Mila to choose whatever she liked, while she herself went in search of a flowerpot and told her son Arnau to carefully dig up the plants.

Mila could still see the lad, tall and straight as a young fir, his legs spread apart and without a care in the world, wielding his fork so skillfully that not one root was broken. The shepherd had told Mila that Arnau, who had come up for military service two years earlier, was now courting a girl in Ridorta and that they'd marry as soon as she reached twenty. Mila imagined what healthy buds would sprout from such sturdy human stock.

Besides the flowers, they had sold her two fertilized eggs and had lent her the hens to hatch them. Mila felt so grateful that often, on her way to and from Murons, she couldn't help peeking in at the farmhouse, where she said hello to everyone as though she had known them all her life. She always found the grandmother, who would urge her to rest awhile by her side before the fire, and Marieta, who would ask her to buy some little item in town: a pennyworth of saffron, a box of cheap matches, some leeches...

Marieta was a tall, gaunt woman. People said she had once been pretty, but the sun, the frost, and the toil of peasant life, not to mention nursing eight children, had quickly put an end to her youth, and her face was now blotchy, while the skin around her eyes and lips was scored with tiny wrinkles that looked as though they had been incised with a knife. Yet her bright eyes, her bustling air and her clear, vibrant voice were so full of good will that everyone loved her.

Shortly after they met, Mila screwed up her courage and asked: "Listen, Marieta, you don't really need so many children to help around the house, but I don't have any and could make such good use of one! How would you feel about lending me Baldiret forever? He's such a comfort up there!"

Marieta smiled. Mila had asked for her nestling, the husband's and grandmother's favorite, and just when it was time to pack him off to school where he'd learn his ABCs... But seeing how crestfallen Mila was, she relented a little and said she could keep him awhile, till she had settled in at the hermitage.

When Mila reached home that morning, she looked everywhere for Matias and, finding him asleep in the shade of the cypresses on the terrace, she roughly pulled his ears.

"Hey lazybones, haven't you heard? I've got some good news... We're going to have a kid..."

Matias turned over and stared at her, while his surprised wife blushed deeply and then, placing her hand on his shoulder, seriously related her conversation with Marieta.

"Ah! God knows what I was thinking!..." And Matias stretched a leg he'd pulled up and closed his eyes again.

Wounded by his indifference, the woman walked away without a word, but all day long she felt grumpy without knowing why, and the next morning she was still in a bad mood. Her fury returned at the sight of Matias leaving the sitting room, a bag over his shoulder and a wooden box with a little glass door around his neck. Inside the box, which was lined with red, velvety paper, upon a pedestal decorated with hackberries and tiny seashells, stood a six-inch statue of St. Pontius, bent and yellow as a consumptive, surrounded by dangling scapulars, shiny little vases of painted roses, and rosaries.

"Where are you going with that?" she exclaimed shrilly, already knowing the answer.

Matias chuckled complacently.

"Well, they say he's a real money-maker... Yesterday Anima told me the last hermit could have made his living just from this."

She burst out: "What difference does that make? Aren't you ashamed, a big healthy man like you, going around begging?"

She spat out the words in a fit of disdainful fury.

Matias was taken off guard, as he always was when she attacked him.

"Me? Well, I have to beg...for the saint."

"For the saint!" and she laughed bitterly. "You know why you want to beg? To keep from getting bored, because even you get sick of lying around all day!... God Almighty! Wasn't it enough for you to make me sell my uncle's house, take me away, and bury me alive in this hole without making me watch you going around with a sack on your back like some good-for-nothing?"

Matias felt very downcast. For twenty-four hours — ever since Anima had aroused him — he'd been dreaming about going out to beg and how much fun and money he'd derive from this new profession. But now his own wife cursed him for entertaining such a thought! All the same, he didn't dare to contradict her. He knew that Mila, like all those who are meek and long-suffering, could silently nurse her grudges for years, but the day her patience ended, the explosion would be violent. He feared such explosions, for he was weak and cowardly, with all the weakness and cowardice of those who are idle. He felt unsure of himself before her, without the wit to dissuade her when she fixed on an idea, and without the strength and decisiveness to change her mind when she was in a temper. So he tried to ride out the storm, but as soon as its fury was spent, his slow, passive determination resurfaced like a buoy.

That day he behaved as was his custom and, covering his retreat with a muttered "Go to the Devil!", he got out of her way and ambled gloomily toward the door.

Matias told Gaietà about their quarrel, and seeing that two days later Mila answered her husband without looking at him, the shepherd tried to think of some way to reconcile them.

A passing shower had forced him to take refuge in the hermitage before lunch. After settling his sheep in the shed and laying out his things, he entered the kitchen with his usual cheerful expression.

"Y'know, hermitess, since it's cool out, we could have a snail picnic. I collected some monsters as big as chestnuts in Wolf Pass, which is where they grow best in these parts. What do you say?"

Mila was delighted, but she'd just finished making lunch.

"Don't worry about a little thing like that. Keep it for supper and you'll have less work to do. With a bowl of soup and these snails, we'll have enough to keep going all day."

Matias also waxed enthusiastic, and the shepherd rubbed his hands together in satisfaction.

"Well then, it's a deal; let's go!... If the hermitess doesn't mind lending me her mortar to make some *aïoli*, because snails without garlic sauce and pepper aren't worth a bean. Hermit, get some kindling from the pile outside the shed and take it to that flat, round lookout that faces south."

Everything stopped for the picnic. As soon as the *aïoli* was ready, the shepherd spooned it onto a red earthenware plate and, followed by Mila with the bread and wineskin, and the boy, who carried a snail basket, he set out for the south slope. The woman could hardly contain her excitement.

"Your snails are tinkling, shepherd!"

"They'll make even sweeter music when we roast them, hermitess."

Matias awaited them on the slope, where he had settled himself beside the pile of kindling, with his legs pulled up, his arms crossed above his knees, and his chin on his arms.

"God damn it, man! You could have laid out the kindling! The *aïoli* 'll melt before we're ready to eat. Go on, make a bed where they can rest easy before they die... The boy and your wife will choose the best-looking ones while I make the forks... I brought some heather specially..."

He emptied his basket onto the ground. Husband and wife burst into admiring exclamations. They couldn't believe the size of those snails: big, dark, with the swirls on their heavy shells half as thick as a finger. Baldiret filled his hands with the handsomest ones. The shepherd looked pleased.

"Pretty good catch, eh? The ones on the plain don't look this good, and for taste there's no comparison. If people down there knew about these snails, the government would have to send troops to protect us!"

They laid them out on the bed of twigs in a spiral pattern, one after the other. Mila and the boy made the selection, while she and Matias set them on the ground, and sometimes, when husband and wife tried to put two snails in the same place, their hands touched and they started laughing, he out of good will, for he wasn't one to bear a grudge, and she without meaning to.

"Get out of there!"

"Hey, mine's bigger!"

When she thought the outer circle was large enough, Mila consulted the shepherd.

"What do you say, Gaietà? Is this enough?"

The shepherd, who squatted nearby sharpening the branches he had just stripped, answered without raising his head.

"Don't stint on the vittles, hermitess... I can shovel it

down with the best of them. I don't like going away half-full, and the boy takes after me. Besides, there's no reason to go easy. We could never eat all the snails around here, and with that shower we just had I reckon I'll find lots more."

"Let's go get them all!" Baldiret shouted.

"You didn't catch my meaning, but I can see you could eat a horse."

So the circle grew, row by row, till it contained all the snails except the cracked or dead ones.

"Now leave it to me!..." and Gaietà, who had finished sharpening the sticks, spread handfuls of twigs on top of the snails till they were well covered. Then he packed the twigs down and lit them.

The fire leapt up instantly.

"Come on, boy! Let's see if you can jump it!"

"Me?" replied Baldiret, his eyes aglow with excitement.

"If you can jump clean over it without getting burnt, I'll give you the snail in the middle, the granddaddy of them all. But if you touch the fire or burn your feet, you won't get a story tonight."

The boy took a few steps backward, spat, pulled up his socks, which were always falling down around his ankles, and, after taking a deep breath, broke into a run.

Mila and the shepherd clapped loudly.

"Did I make it?" asked Baldiret, stumbling unsteadily after his leap.

"No question! You were at least an inch above the flame!" exclaimed the laughing shepherd. "You won the granddaddy, all right. After you eat it, we'll hang the shell around the ram's neck so it'll jingle."

The blaze began to die down, crackling here and there, and beneath the crackle you could hear the sizzle of roasting snails.

"Listen to them hissing, poor things," Mila mumbled.

"Don't be sad, hermitess. Everything has to die when

its time comes, and don't think they were having much fun before. They hadn't eaten in over a month. Come on now, let's get the tools ready...they're starting to smell good."

They gathered the bread, wine, *aïoli*, and those four pointed sticks.

"Let's see how they look now." The shepherd approached the fire, lifted some burning twigs, and peered at the snails beneath them.

"Those souls in torment are still begging for more, hissing and sputtering like sinners in Purgatory. Take a good look at your side, hermit."

Since the snails on Matias' side were almost done, he shifted the fire toward the shepherd, while a penetrating smell of charred shells and cooking snails spread through the nearby fields.

When the flames had died down and only an occasional tongue flickered among the ashes, what remained was a black circle dotted with glowing lumps.

"Boy, get up close; it's our turn now. Let's see who blows harder."

And on their hands and knees, stretching their necks and shutting their eyes, the shepherd and his lad huffed and puffed to clear away the ashes and glowing bits of twigs.

"Oh no! They're all burned!" cried Mila as soon as they saw the shells, some of which were whitened and others blackened by the fire, and all of which resembled toy cinnamon buns in a dollhouse.

"Don't be so sure, hermitess. May I never win a raffle if there aren't a hundred good ones here!"

They blew and picked out bits of straw and twigs till the spiral was clean but continuous like a single strip, for the snails were soldered together with dark, sticky paste.

"Dingaling! It's the dinner bell, ladies and gentlemen! Come and get it while it's hot!"

And the shepherd, pushing his cap back and clapping his hands, sat down beside the circle and crossed his legs.

"Let me have a stick!" cried Mila.

"Where should we put the *aïoli*?" asked Matias, holding the plate in his hand.

"Where we all can reach it... Here, near the snails... Hey, let the boy have that big one in the middle... He won it with his leap."

The boy picked up the shell, whose mouth oozed yellowish-green liquid.

"Look! Look!" he exclaimed, holding it out to the shepherd.

"I bet that one cursed a lot before giving up the ghost. That's why its mouth is so dirty... But don't break it; remember, I want to hang it on the ram."

They were all seated, and four hands, one on each side, broke up the spiral. Their heather sticks nosily poked around in the shells, skillfully digging out the green snails that ended in muddy white twists and that were then dunked in *aïoli* and greedily devoured.

The outer rings of the spiral quickly disappeared, while Mussol, the shepherd's dog, prowled around the four eaters, picking up empty shells, licking them, and noisily grinding them between his teeth.

"Praise be to God! Fasting is good for the health...can you taste how sweet they are? Boy, if you save those shells, on St. Pontius' Day I'll make a bunch of tiny lanterns you can put out on the terrace."

Mila couldn't help exclaiming: "Shepherd, there's nothing you can't do!"

He chortled.

"If you want some more, I'll meet you in Wolf Pass this afternoon. Then you'll see what we can do together..."

A piercing warble, like a canary's song, came from directly below them, and the curious picnickers turned to look down.

A man approached, whistling and waving his arms as he walked.

Matias shouted: "Anima!... Hey, Anima!..."

The man raised his head, peered at them, and then shut his eyes and showed his teeth. Mila immediately recognized the peasant who'd asked her for a drink.

Without haste, Anima walked on till he reached them.

"*Hoo hoo hoo*, I knew you were roasting snails as soon as I saw the fire and my nose started twitching like a greyhound's. *Hoo, hoo!* What a smell!"

"Want to try one? They're tasty as can be!" said Matias, moving over to make room for him.

The man hesitated, but encouraged by Matias' second invitation and Mila's laughter, he squatted on his heels.

Since there was no stick for him, he pulled out his horn-handled knife, whose short, wide blade was as sharp as a dagger. Though he held the weapon, he almost always cracked the shells between his teeth like green almonds and, after spitting out the pieces, swallowed the snails. This technique turned Mila's stomach, though the man did occasionally use his knife to dunk the snails in *aïoli*, whereupon she noticed that his hands were long, thin, blackened and covered with thick, uneven hair, as though they had recently been scorched in a fire.

As soon as the man appeared, Gaietà fell silent and quietly went on eating, but every time he raised the wineskin his eyes flashed at their guest.

Suddenly Mila cried: "We forgot the soup!"

The shepherd turned to her.

"You're right, by God!... Well, that just goes to show we didn't need it in the first place...and we won't miss it after a feed like this one... I'm full, anyhow."

At that point Mila caught an answering flash beneath Anima's thick brows, but it died away immediately. The man's eyes were shut and he was laughing that bizarre laugh of his.

"*Hoo hoo hoo!...* Can I have one for the wife?"

They stared at him in amazement.

Then he pulled a rope around his chest till a tangled net appeared holding a tawny object: it was a ferret he'd been keeping behind his back.

Baldiret's eyes grew big as saucers, and he could hardly sit still.

The animal restlessly pawed the net and sniffed, poking its white snout through the holes.

Anima crushed a snail, spat out the shell, and offered the meat to his ferret.

"It eats snails too?" asked Matias.

"Everything except eggs, 'cause I'd have to pay for 'em." The man shut his eyes and laughed, as was his custom.

"Where have I seen him before?" Mila wondered.

"It's fun hunting with a ferret," said Matias.

"So they say... *Hoo hoo hoo...* Come along this afternoon and you'll see."

Matias began to get excited.

"Are you going far?"

"Only to Three Comb Gorge..."

"Sure. Why not? There's nothing to do at the hermitage."

Mila's brow suddenly furrowed.

"Weren't you going to work on the terrace today?"

"I'll do it tomorrow...we've got plenty of time."

Baldiret clung to the shepherd's shoulder, rubbing against it a little.

"What is it?"

The boy slowly whispered, without taking his eyes off the ferret: "Can I go too?"

The shepherd looked at him seriously.

"That's not for you, son. When you're older..."

"Aw! Let him go... He can carry the rabbits, can't you, Baldiret?" Matias cheerfully interjected.

The boy looked again at the shepherd, who would have liked to say no, but those big green eyes begged so tenderly that he hadn't the heart to refuse.

"Okay, just this once,"he reluctantly agreed, thinking: "I'll make sure you won't ask again."

When the last snail had disappeared and the three hunters were on their way down the slope, the shepherd, holding Mussol's collar to keep the dog from following them, turned to Mila, who was still seated by the circle of ashes, and said, shaking his head: "We're in for trouble, hermitess! That bird of ill omen is circling round your home. I'm telling you again: watch out, watch out! It's no laughing matter, I can promise you."

"But who is he?"

"Who is he? God knows! Who can tell where that bastard came from? They say he used to beg with an old man when he was little, and when the old man died he worked in some of the farmhouses, but they all threw him out for being so sneaky. Now he poaches rabbits instead of working. He'll hunt them all year long till there's none left in these hills. He can't stand me because I won't let him get away with it. When I see he's got his eye on a burrow, I plant a scarecrow in front of it so the rabbits'll get scared and move. But I have to look sharp, 'cause if he caught me he'd make me pay for it. Look: he used to have a gun. I told you I like to walk in the fog. Well, one day when I was up on Goblin Crest, which is so clean and quiet you can hear a pin drop a mile away, a bullet whizzed by my ear. I couldn't see a soul, because there was nothing but white clouds, but may God strike me dead if it wasn't that rascal! He finally made so much trouble that the Civil Guard took his gun away, but I still wouldn't trust him as far as I could throw him. He knows everything that's going on, how to imitate all kinds of animals, and he always thinks he's one or another of them. How else could it be, when you think about it? Did you see those monkey paws? He's more beast than man."

A thought suddenly struck Mila.

"Wait a minute! Now I know where I've seen him! It's not that I ever laid eyes on him, but he's got the same teeth and gums as a bitch my uncle had when I was little. Exactly the same..." And looking at the shepherd in amazement, she whispered: "You're right. He's more beast than man!"

VI. Tales

In the spring evenings, which were still cool in the mountains, everyone gathered in Mila's kitchen. Each time they threw a new kermes log on the fire, a red bouquet burst forth, bending its bright tongues as if before an equinoctial tempest, casting fierce, shifting reflections upon the shadowy walls, and surrounding the shepherd and his lad with fiery auras, like demons in a mystery play.

The boy sat by the woodpile, periodically feeding that diminutive inferno, while Gaietà, his cap pushed back, stripped hackberry switches that would later serve as collars for errant rams, walking sticks for proud farmboys coming of age, and whistling whips for the wagoners in Murons. Matias usually stretched out on the bench beside the table, gazing upward with his hands folded behind his head, while Mila bustled around, preparing the meal and listening, or – when she could – sitting awhile by the fire.

As the shepherd whittled, he told stories to Baldiret, and his soft voice, suffused with the lilt of his distant birthplace, filled the cozy room with its simple, druidic majesty. The first story Mila heard was the one about the fairy echoes.

So let it serve as an example.

The shepherd began: "Once upon a time, when the animals could still talk, an old, old man dwelt in these mountains for centuries. Such was the will of God, who let him live longer than other men because he'd never sinned or touched a woman in all his days. Instead of breeches and a jacket, he wore only his hair, which was so long and thick that it hid his back like a cape, and his white beard, which hung all the way down to his knees."

Baldiret cried out in wonder, and the shepherd cheerfully replied: "Now if we went around like that, we'd make a pretty picture, wouldn't we? But to get back to the old man, he was a hermit who did nothing but pray day and night, and he ate only roots, with an occasional hackberry as a special treat."

"Hackberries?" asked the boy, whose surprise was now even greater since he often ate them himself.

"That's what I said! Maybe they were even from that tree in the ravine where we cut sticks every time we pass by."

Baldiret marveled at the thought, while the shepherd continued: "The old man was so holy that other people kept away from him so God wouldn't notice what a big difference there was. One by one, his neighbors moved down to the plain till finally there was no one left except that old man and the fairies. I already told you how Badblood Creek, Three Comb Gorge and the caves near Flatrock had more fairies than a dog has fleas. But you can't see fairies, so people would walk right through a crowd of them, thinking they were all alone. Imagine how the little people laughed fit to burst! And don't forget, fairies love to fool around, and that's how all this trouble started. Because once everyone had left, they didn't know what to do for fun. They got grouchier and grouchier and lonelier and lonelier till finally they realized it was all that root-eating old man's fault. Determined to get even, they called a meeting in that ravine near the Nina. Everyone said her say, but there were so many they just couldn't seem to reach an agreement...fairies, you know, can talk a blue streak. And they never would have done anything if all of a sudden the littlest one, who was very naughty, hadn't leapt up and said: 'Now wait a minute, ladies! I've been thinking how to make a holy man lose his soul, and if you'll leave it to me I'll take care of everything.' They all agreed, and the next morning at daybreak, when the old man was saying his prayers, he saw a big shadow in front of him. He looked up, and you'll never guess what he saw! A little golden bird with three feathers on its crest, as red and shiny as three drops of blood."

The boy's green eyes shone like twin lanterns, and his hands forgot to feed the fire. The shepherd began to strip another stick.

"The old man was charmed by the little bird and stared so long that he forgot his Paternoster. When the bird flew away toward Highpeak, the man scratched his head and wondered: 'How could something so tiny cast such a big shadow when the sun isn't even out? And another thing: what kind of bird was that? I've never seen the like in all my born days! Was it a hoopoe? Was it a starling? Was it a swift? Was it a greenfinch?' But no matter how long he thought, he couldn't recollect anything like it."

The shepherd stopped to cut off a shoot, which landed in the fire and made it flare up, momentarily revealing his two listeners' attentive faces. Even Matias, who was half-asleep on the bench, stirred, rubbed his back against the wood, and opened a curious eye to see why Gaietà had fallen silent, for the human voice so enchants us that when it stops, we long for its return.

But the shepherd's stories were never interrupted for long; they flowed generously, like water from a bubbling spring.

"The old man, who was as innocent as a babe in arms, would never have dreamed anyone was out to fool him. But I bet you can guess those fairies were up to no good. And sure enough, as soon as he knelt the next morning, he saw that same shadow and the same little bird, except that this time it didn't just hop around and chirp but warbled as prettily as the sweetest nightingale. Like I said, this old man was as innocent as a child, and kids are like monkeys – they want to touch whatever they see. So as soon as he could, he reached out to touch the little bird, but when it saw what he wanted, lickety split! It flew off toward Highpeak. And you know what the old man did then? He forgot to pray, dig for roots, or even chew on a dried hackberry. At night, instead of sleeping, he could only think of one thing: that bird, that little golden bird. So while the stars played hide-and-seek, the old man was kneeling in the same spot with a slipknot he'd made, and when the sun came out and that bird returned, he tossed out his rope and..."

"Did he catch it?"

"Right around the neck, and once he had it, the old man laughed and said:

Well well, little friend,
I caught you in the end.

"But he almost turned to stone when the little bird replied:

Please, dear old man,
Spare me if you can.

" 'A Moorish king bewitched me and gave me to the fairies, but the spell can be broken by one who's never touched a woman.'

"The old man's heart leapt up when he heard these words, for he thought Our Lord wanted him to perform a miracle never seen before. So he answered:

Little golden bird,
You can trust my word.

" 'I promise to free you, since I'm an old man and have never touched a woman. Now tell me quickly what I must do.'

" 'Pull two feathers from my crest,' the bird replied, 'and stick them in your eyes.' The old man did as he was told, and no sooner had he stuck the feathers in his eyes than he turned blind as a bat. 'Oh dear, what have I done?' he cried. 'I'll never see again!' But the bird laughed and laughed, and when it had finished laughing, it plucked the last feather from its crest and pierced the man's heart. The light returned to his eyes, and you'll never guess what he saw before him."

Baldiret was so enthralled that he forgot to speak.

"Well, he saw a girl as pretty as the Holy Virgin, but as naked as he was. All she wore was a garland of roses around her neck, hanging down to her feet..."

The shepherd interrupted himself to ask: "Well, who do you think that girl was?"

"The fairy!"

"Right! And the roses?"

Baldiret looked up and down, rubbed his cheek against his shoulder, but...he couldn't figure out what those roses might be.

"The slipknot!"

"Oh..." And the boy bit his tongue in annoyance at not thinking of something so simple.

"So what happened?" Mila eagerly asked.

"Listen and I'll tell you. Those fairies know what they're up to, and the poor old holy man had never seen anything so lovely! When he caught sight of that girl standing there staring at him, he blushed from head to toe, pulled his hair around him, and covered his face with his hands, but he'd forgotten the main thing: to pull the magic feather out of his heart. So no matter how he hid his face, it was like his hands were made of glass and he kept seeing that fairy before him till finally she said,

Old man who before me stands,
Now take away your hands.

" 'I mean you no harm, for I, Dawnflower, the smallest fairy in the gorge, have taken pity on you. If you'll come with me, I'll make you the richest man alive. Behind the Roar, we'll find the entrance to my mountain palace of stardust and seashells. Its towers are coral, its doors are silver, and its columns are bones from Crunchnoggin, the giant my father slew because he wanted to marry me. There you'll sleep on a canopied gold bed in a mirrored chamber hung with jeweled damask, eat fish from underground milky rivers, and drink mead blended daily by the King of Orient's three hundred wives...'

"The fairy stopped there, thinking he had plenty of reason to follow her. But the old man, who'd regained his senses and prayed to God for strength, suddenly turned away and cried: 'Get thee hence, wicked witch, for I prize Heaven above such riches!' The fairy shot him a nasty look and vanished into thin air."

Baldiret's long face revealed his disappointment. How could a man with no more clothing than his hair refuse a palace made of glittering stardust, with coral towers and silver doors?

"So did the fairy come back?"

"The old man hardly knew what hit him. He tried walking from the Roar to the Cliff and from Cockfoot to Roepass, saying his prayers and doing penance as he went. But he couldn't get the fairy out of his mind, with that hair like gold dust and those roses around her neck. By midnight he couldn't stand it any more and knelt in the same place, but although he waited and waited, he saw neither girl nor bird. Then he thought: 'If only she'd come back, I'd cover her with my hair, for no young lady should run about like that.' No sooner had he thought it than she appeared, but instead of giving her his hair, he just glanced at her, lowered his eyes, and started trembling. Then the fairy said: 'Though you drove me away yesterday, pity has brought me back. Since you spurn my riches, I shall make you the mightiest man alive. I'll give you armor of flint, a lightning sword, and a horse swifter than the wind. Thus clad, armed, and mounted you can conquer the world, nor will anyone stop you, for if they smite your suit, a ray of fire will burst forth; if they try to flee, your horse will catch them; and if they refuse to surrender, your flaming sword will turn them to ashes.'

"Her words filled the old man with sadness and doubt, and seeing this, she asked what he was thinking. The old man took a great leap and said in a terrified voice: 'Get thee hence, wicked witch, for I prize Heaven above such might!' Feeling even more annoyed than the first day, she kicked the ground and vanished into thin air."

The shepherd stopped to stretch his arms and scratch his head, but the boy's impatience would not let him rest long.

"So...?"

"Hold on, I'm out of breath. You know, story-telling's not like running a race. Well, after spurning Dawn-flower's second offer, the old man felt sadder than a new widow and spent the whole day weeping and thinking to himself: 'It must be a lot nicer to have a mountain palace, sleep in a canopied bed, eat fish from milky rivers, and drink mead from the Orient than to sleep in caves or in the damp, cut your feet on brambles, and live on nothing but bitter roots and water. But I'm just a poor sinner and God has offered me nothing better, for He surely knows how little I deserve.' This idea calmed him for a while, but then he thought: 'Even so, it did sound good what that fairy said: to ride through the world ruling lands that take my fancy. You can cross these mountains in four days, but the world must be a lot bigger. Maybe it takes ten or twelve days to cross it, or even as many as all my toes and fingers together. When I was little, a crow once told me there were as many kinds of men as birds, and each kind spoke a different tongue and had different-colored feathers. That would be a sight to see, but I guess that crow was lying. He'd been all over, and I've never left these hills. When I was young, I should have traveled and seen a bit of the world... It's not much fun spending your life like a lizard in a hole.' And while he chewed over these thoughts that had never crossed his mind before, night fell, and before sunrise he knelt in the same place to await the fairy. He was certain she'd come back and, though he'd hardened his heart against her, he also felt impatient, for all men love company."

"And did she come back?" asked Mila.

"Even earlier than the other days. Before daybreak she appeared at his side, sitting there with eyes brighter than Mussol's and saying in a voice even sweeter than when she'd been a bird: 'Alas, dear old man, you must have bewitched me, for despite your cruelty I cannot forsake you. Come what may, I have decided to reward your kindness, and as you spurn power and riches, I'll make you the wisest man alive. You'll know everything that happens on earth and in Heaven. You'll see the sap rise in tree trunks and how leaves and flowers grow. You'll see ants burrowing on the other side of the globe and ships upon the ocean. You'll see pathways between stars and caverns in Hell, full of vile beasts and souls in torment, writhing and clawing, and you'll see the plottings of men's minds and children in their mothers' wombs. From east to west, all will be open to your gaze... You'll hear and understand everything too: what birds and beasts say, the songs fishes sing, mermaids beneath the sea, the howling wind, the rumbling thunder, the moaning mountains, and every sound made by anything near or far... You'll know all the world's secrets and how to seek good and shun evil.' As the fairy spoke, the old man stared and his heart filled with longing.

" 'Whatever shall I do?' he thought to himself. 'Should I heed her words? Should I follow her? If I refuse I'll die of sorrow, but if I go I'll burn in Hell, for I know fairies' powers are nothing but wickedness. Alas, I've already damned my soul by looking and listening.' Meanwhile, the fairy watched him and finally said: 'Well, I've offered you everything I possess. Now tell me once and for all: will you come away or not?' The old man wept and cried aloud: 'Get thee hence, wicked witch, for I can stand no more!' And burying his head between his knees, he prayed God to give him strength, but she approached the old man and whispered in his ear: 'Oh beloved, please come, for my sole wish is to make you the richest, mightiest, and wisest man alive.' The old man covered his ears and cried out with all his might: 'No, no! Get away, evil spirit, for I prize Heaven above all this world's wonders!' As soon as he had spoken, everything darkened like on Judgment Day, and he thought the fairy had fled again."

"And had she?" asked Mila, whose eyes were big as saucers.

"No indeed, hermitess! She hadn't finished her day's work, and I told you she wasn't one to leave a job half-done. Seeing how stubborn the old man was, she put her arm around his neck and said slowly, as if she was at Confession: 'Well, I fear I shall never sway one so saintly and pure of heart. You had won my love and I hoped to make you my husband, but now you have spurned me thrice, and so I must depart. Never again will you see, hear, or learn of my doings, but first I shall leave you something to remember me by as long as the world endures.' And so saying, she drew nearer, gave him a long kiss, and vanished into thin air."

"And she never came back?"

"No, hermitess, this time she stayed away. Otherwise the story would never end." The shepherd looked at Mila's face and laughed.

"What?" she cried in astonishment. "You mean that's all?"

"Everything but the moral, but don't complain till you hear the end. As soon as she'd left the old man, Dawnflower mounted a passing breeze, which swiftly bore her to Deadwoman's Gorge. There she saw the other fairies gossiping while they knitted, and as soon as she caught sight of them, she shouted as loud as she could:

Oh fairy sisters on this wondrous day,
Throw your foolish knitting away!
Take up your diamond combs of old,
Your moon-mirrors of flaming gold,
And your necklaces of serpent-eyes
That provoke the blindman's cries.
Lily-robes will now be worn
That you with salmon-scales adorn,
And your satin slippers you must don,
For men will come anon!

"Imagine what a fuss they all made! The fairies asked and asked how it had happened, till finally Dawnflower told them exactly what she'd done. The fairies, who couldn't believe their ears, listened to how she'd tempted him, and hearing that she had vainly offered riches, might, and wisdom, which are usually the best baits to trap a man and steal his soul, but that their littlest sister had bested him all the same, they asked what tools, chains, potions or spells had done it. Finally she told them: she'd damned his soul with a single kiss! For ever since the world began, no potion, chain, trick, jailer, or spell could bewitch a man like a woman's kiss. Some of the sillier ones started laughing at her words, but just then they heard a low muffled voice, like a wave breaking deep within the forest. They listened closely till they heard what it said: 'Dawnflower! Dawnflower! Dawnflower!' It was the old man, running to and fro, first to Goblin Crest, then to King's Glass, then to Olivebreath, searching for the fairy and begging her to return, offering his very soul for just one more kiss. The fairies were delighted and fanned out through the mountains, laughing, mocking, and repeating his words. And that's how they got that bad habit they still have today."

"And what became of the old man, shepherd?"

"He died of a broken heart before that century was out, and since he passed away in a state of sin, he couldn't go to Heaven...may God pity him! And even now, hermitess, on stormy nights, when Highpeak's bones rattle to show someone's in trouble, you can see his wandering soul, like a will-o'-the-wisp in the gorges and glens, and his voice, dark and drawn out like the echo of a wave, keeps crying 'Dawnflower! Dawnflower! Dawnflower!' till daybreak comes."

VII. Spring

The beginning of May was wonderful. The mountains, fragrant with new flowers, bathed in sunlight, and full of warbling birds, lost their savage, millennial aspect and seemed to regain their youth, with all youth's gaiety in budding courtship. Every morning Mila awoke to some new delight she had overlooked the day before, and moreover, she herself also seemed to grow younger. Her eyes, which had been melancholy, recovered their old sparkle, while her lips reddened, her breasts swelled like a young mother's, and a light, graceful harmony pervaded her movements. These outward changes corresponded to a rush of feelings so volatile that at times she felt herself multiplying into dozens of different women. It seemed that a mysterious inner light constantly altered her complexion, like those distant mountains that changed from hour to hour. The others also noted a change in Mila.

One day Gaietà affectionately said: "Hermitess, I bet you don't have a bad word left to say about St. Pontius. It's a miracle how much better you look. Why, you were skinny as a rail when I first laid eyes on you, and now you're the prettiest thing I ever saw alive!"

Another day, Arnau from St. Pontius' Farm went hunting and stopped in as he passed the hermitage to say hello.

"Anyone home?" he called out from the front gate.

"Who's there? Come on up!" Mila shouted down from the kitchen, and, leaving the dishes half-washed, went onto the balcony and leaned over the railing.

Arnau stopped halfway up the stairs and, after hesitating a moment, exclaimed: "My God! I hardly recognized you... You look like a new woman..."

While he was there, Mila bustled about without looking straight at him, but she saw that his admiring gaze never left her.

On still another afternoon so sultry that it felt like mid-August, she took her sewing basket and sat down in the shade of an almond tree, where she began to mend one of Matias' shirts. In the distance she could see the mountains and, far away on her right, the Husk rose up beneath a brilliant blue sky. Four steps from her on the left, a row of bushes bounded the little orchard, and above her the almond tree spread its branches, heavy with all those nuts the shepherd had predicted. Under that green canopy, so thick the sun's rays could barely penetrate it, the temperature was far lower than in the sweltering fields. The coolness soon made Mila, who had risen early and whom the muggy heat had affected, want to lie down, and without taking her sewing off her lap, she lay back on the sloping ground behind her. In her bosom, hot like the day, she felt the buried life stirring, her eyes were dazzled by the dark greens and translucent undersides of leaves, and a longing to stretch her muscles made her fling her arms wide so that they rested, palms up, beside her on the grass, while the sluggish blood flowed slowly through her veins. She dozed off in this position, but in the course of her nap the god of sleep mischievously tugged at her blouse, whose top two buttons she had undone, and stretched one of her legs till its foot rested against the other. Her head was thrown back, her mouth was half open, and her white neck emerged from the blouse's bluish depths, which revealed the softly rounded contours of her breasts... She slept deeply, motionlessly, but suddenly, as though troubled by a bad dream, she began to show signs of agitation. Her body stirred, her brow furrowed, her right arm twitched convulsively, her face, pale in repose, reddened slightly... Mila opened her eyes, blinked, looked around, and...abruptly sat up. Two sparks glinted among the bushes: two wolfish eyes pierced her like glowing needles.

"*Hoo hoo hoo...* The ferret gave me the slip. *Hoo hoo hoo...*" And Anima, trampling blackberry bushes and laughing that guttural laugh of his, slowly backed away from her till he was out of sight. After he was gone, Mila kept staring into the brambles, listening to her pounding heart, still seeing those glittering eyes and sharp white teeth. Then she suddenly bent forward, buried her head between her thighs, and clutched her knees. A heady mixture of shame, joy, fear, and desire crept over her, rising from her feet to her head like a whirlpool and nearly causing her to faint.

When she recovered, she felt groggy, her spine was cold, and the pattern of little holes on her thimble was imprinted on her left arm.

She picked up her sewing basket and slowly set off for home.

As usual, Matias had said he was going to visit the rector, and this reminded Mila that she hadn't been to Confession and really ought to go. Yes, she should go, but what was there to confess?

For days now, stifled rages, strange flashes of exuberance, disappointments with she scarcely knew what, secret, uncertain shudders had passed over her like shooting stars or black bumblebees, but were these sometimes vivid, sometimes vague impressions really sins to be confessed? She thought not; they weren't for a priest but for another sort of person... "The shepherd!" she suddenly thought, following the logic of her musings... But she blushed as soon as the idea occurred to her: "No! No! Certainly not the shepherd! Why not? Well...

because!" The shepherd was so unworldly... If she told him about her feelings, he wouldn't understand... He might laugh, and then again he might look at her differently. He thought St. Pontius could cure anything, he shared none of her moods, he once had called her a heretic, he seemed to live in his own fantasies... No, not the shepherd! Matias would have been better, if he were another sort of man, a man like those others who really looked at her: with Arnau's admiring gaze, for example, or Anima's goatish leer, or even with Mussol's moist and faithful eyes...like a man or beast, but with some kind of response. Matias had no distinctive look, she now realized for the first time. He had no look because peace reigned within him, as in a peaceful animal but an abnormal one, more bestial than the others because he was never in rut.

This abnormality, once recognized, pursued and gnawed at Mila like the memory of some misdeed, something that made her life seem sordid and miserable. And with secret shame, though unconsciously, she began to bend all her efforts toward making things once again as they should be. To her surprise and consternation, she found herself acting like a playful kitten, adopting suggestive poses, feigned languors, seductive intonations, fluttering lashes, quiet sighs...an entire arsenal of amorous arms hitherto unused by her and that she now wielded with the bitter fury of a woman scorned... But upon seeing that not even these weapons could open the desired breach and that all remained quiet in the opposing camp, she felt defeated and longed to drag herself along the ground, to bite her own flesh, to crawl into a corner and starve to death, to transform her troubled self into something numb, stony, unaware... "If only I could be like them," she thought, standing outside the hermitage and watching the Ridorta women come down the mountain like a column of ants, each one bent beneath a bundle of firewood three times her size, without desires, yearnings, consciousness, or any other thought than the weight they bore upon their backs, but that all the same was not so heavy as the one inside Mila. In her mind, she reconstructed their daily routine: to get up in the dark, gather ropes and sacks, meet the other women and together climb the mountain in the cool morning air, repeating neighborhood gossip, dirty jokes, wonderful tales like the shepherd's. Once there, they would uproot kermes oak after kermes oak, stuff their sacks, hoist those heavy crosses onto their backs and head for Murons, where they delivered their bundles to the bakers and received a couple of pennies before returning home, exhausted but glad to have survived another day.

Mila then stopped short in the middle of her imaginings... Despite everything, those women's lives were not sufficiently calm, boring, or dead. Better to be a plant, free of all servitude, need, toil and anxiety...or better still, a hard, stony mountain like the Roquís.

Now a creature to which she had always been indifferent or even hostile found a place in her heart. She grew fond of a baby lamb whose fleece was white as a cloud. She fed it breadcrumbs, while the lamb followed her like a puppy, climbed onto her lap, and took lettuce leaves from her mouth. A shiver of delight ran through Mila when she felt that warm, silky muzzle on her face and smelled its breath against her skin. The lamb's gaze was as stupid as Matias', but so much more tender and innocent! Whenever the lamb looked at her, Mila felt like crying.

Other pets, however, soon displaced the lamb.

One day the shepherd came back acting very upset.

At St. Pontius' Farm, they had driven away a cat that ate their chickens and that at last had taken refuge in a nearby gorge, where it hunted wild birds with consummate skill. In that gorge, it had born four kittens as wild and calico as itself. One day Anima saw them, trapped the cat, tortured it awhile for his amusement, and finally kicked it to death. Then he went cheerfully on his way, squinting and baring his gums. When the four kittens grew hungry, they approached their mother and sucked at the dead cat's nipples. The next morning they were meowing disconsolately.

Baldiret saw it all and told the shepherd, who then repeated the story to Mila: "And I swear I'll make that bastard pay for what he's done. By tomorrow night all the burrows he's watching will be empty. To starve those poor little kittens! He should have hit them with a rock and put them out of their misery."

Mila shuddered, and that afternoon she, Gaietà, and Baldiret went to the gorge. As they approached, they heard the kittens crying and saw the four of them, looking as bristly as hedgehogs, flee as fast as their rickety little legs could carry them. Gentle calls and enticements proved useless. The wild creatures, hidden in the underbrush, refused to be lured forth or to let anyone approach them. For three or four days Mila had her work cut out for her. Every morning and evening she visited the gorge, where she left gifts of food for the kittens. One refused to eat and starved to death, but the other three allowed her to collect them, more dead than alive, and take them back to the hermitage. Through care and patience, she was able to save two, who became more revered and exalted than the sacred cats of ancient Egypt. Anyone who tried to harm them would have seen Mila in a rage hitherto unknown. But the kittens throve, hunted for food, played all day and no longer needed her. Then her heart felt as barren as before and again longed to give itself unstintingly.

One day, as she was trying some suspenders on Baldiret, the same glow that had invaded her on their first visit to the Roar again swept through her. She suddenly seized the boy's head, pressed her face against it, and covered him with famished kisses... The lad blinked and shrank beneath that amorous onslaught, as surprised and disconcerted as a bird fallen from its nest. From that day on, Baldiret illumined Mila's dark loneliness, and, happier and more pampered than if he had been her natural son, he could not say whom he loved more: her or the shepherd.

VIII. The Festival of Roses

For the first time since her arrival, Mila took the path she had used to ascend the mountain. She had always gone down the Murons side, but after hearing how good the eggs and lettuce in Ridorta were, she set out to order some for St. Pontius' festival.

It was early morning, but the sun, already far above the Husk, streaked the distant hills with its rays.

Taking small steps, Mila absentmindedly made her way down the gully, as smooth as a giant wheeltrack, thinking thoughts as vague as the drifting clouds above her.

Below lay the clearing around the Boundary Stone, circular as a frying pan, with its jugged handle – the second stretch of Legbreak Creek – attached at an angle. When she left the gully to start the second stretch, she remembered Matias' words: "Your feet can't stop, and before you know, it's over." Indeed, Mila felt like she was sliding down a banister and almost immediately found herself where she had stopped that first day. An old man with a dirty sack over his shoulder was resting in the same spot. Mila greeted him and continued on toward the Boundary Stone, eager to see the plain again from above.

Cautiously selecting footholds and rocks to hang onto, she clambered up the steps and gazed out upon the scene below, as majestic and astonishing as it had been before.

The plain was full of rosy blotches clustered so thickly that if one squinted a little it looked entirely pink. "Holy Virgin! It's so pretty!" thought Mila, awed once more.

Beneath that bright blue sky, the hill, flecked with spring green, covered with white houses, and encircled at its base by a band of rosy gauze, was more like a painter's luminous vision than something real and palpable.

But what was all that pink below her? Mila decided to ask the man, who was still resting.

"Those are St. Pontius' roses, waiting to be blessed. Now the fields are full of them, but the day after tomorrow there won't be one left. They'll all go up the mountain."

Mila soon learned that he had spoken the truth.

Awakening at four, she beheld a trickle of early risers, human rosebushes, fragrant bouquets that opened in the morning air. Later, as the day progressed, the bouquets multiplied and grew thicker, coming from all sides along pathways and trails, past grottoes and over crests, by brooks and Cockfoot's cliffs. By ten the entire mountain looked like an immense garden. The bells in the steeple rang frantically, joyously summoning the crowd, and the crowd, feeling that gaiety surge through its eyes and hearts, its expansive gestures and resounding voices, kept on, holding those magic roses that in their death throes garlanded everything: land, air, and human spirits.

From the bouquet's dense center, the fields around the hermitage, rose a buzz of cries, laughter, whispers, curses, songs...the festival's sonorous breath.

Everyone in the area, from Llisquents to the sea and from Roquesalbes to the distant plain, congregated on the barren slopes around St. Pontius' Hermitage, which, unable to hold them all, overflowed toward the Roar, toward nearby pine groves and streams where people gathered in restless clumps and picturesque encampments. By mid-morning they were everywhere, mysterious parts of some strategic plan: circles of stones around fires, baskets and panniers emptied onto the ground, and later, numerous white columns of smoke, cutting through the still air like misty trees in a forest of mirages. The path from Murons could accomodate, though not very well, horses and even rented buggies, provided they were pulled by stout hooves and used by passengers accustomed to bumps and jolts. Vendors came by that same route with wares on their backs or packed on mules, bearing pastries and sweets, glazed fruit, white wine and liquor, toasted almonds and pine nuts, perfume bottles and glass jars, tin soldiers and brass trumpets, games of skill and chance. A blind violinist sang whining melodies about notorious crimes of passion, and Cristòfol, the village idiot from Llisquents, grimaced and gesticulated amidst circles of onlookers, for whom he mimicked every known beast from nightingale to hog, from ass to lizard.

The vendors gathered in the yard by the hermitage and, lined up beneath the cypresses, laid out their wares, which they hawked to a gaping, good-humored crowd mainly composed of the old and very young in their Sunday best: stiff jackets and breeches handed down by their fathers, long skirts that kept tripping the little girls, who wore bright kerchiefs on their heads, while the boys sported caps whose scarlet was so brilliant that the yard seemed speckled with fiery cinnabar.

Mila, who had never seen such a gathering, was dazzled and dismayed. She had visited the steeple a half dozen times to get them to stop ringing, but although her head was about to split, no one paid any attention. A horde of children and teenagers, bored with looking at stalls and performers, and pushing their way up and down the stairs to the hermitage, had conquered the belfry, where they reigned despotically. Dangling in clusters from the ropes, they rang ceaselessly, and those who found no rope to seize hung from the high windows, waving their arms in feigned terror, laughing and calling out to the indifferent multitude. The head of this excited throng was Baldiret, his clothing rumpled and his hair on end, who

flew here and there with a shriek on his lips. He was so
beside himself that upon seeing him, Mila abandoned her
plan to scold the lad and try to restore order in the
belfry.

She herself felt unnerved by all the noise and scarcely
knew where to turn. She went from balcony to courtyard,
courtyard to kitchen, kitchen to terrace, through boisterous mobs that pursued her, demanding this and that.
From time immemorial, the hermitage had rented
cooking utensils at a modest price, sold eggs, oil, lettuce,
white wine and anisette, and served cooked food to those
too lazy to prepare it. Flanked by batteries of pots,
casseroles, and saucepans, two cooks from Murons and
their assistants, knives in hand, fiercely attacked chickens,
ducks, and geese, who squawked and fluttered in terror
before surrendering to their fate.

Anima had promised to supply the rabbits. The
previous evening he had brought in eleven, some with
heads crushed by rocks or his boots and others with
haunches gnawed by the ferret. But, aware that a dozen
would never suffice, he had promised to bring more the
next day. And that morning Mila saw him by the hearth,
skinning rabbits like a magician who could pull them from
a hat.

From time to time men and women would enter the
kitchen.

"You couldn't sell us something to eat, could you?"

Anima would offer the beast he was skinning, for
which they bargained and paid. He put aside the pelt,
and an instant later, another rabbit would hang by its
hind foot from a hook beneath the mantel.

Mila couldn't help stopping a moment to contemplate
that implacable process, for she had never seen such agile
hands. With one swift incision, he cut around the hind
legs, left them clad in their soft raiment, gripped the knife
between his teeth, and grasping that gray cassock lined

with membrane thin and glistening as a slice of onion, quickly pulled it down, leaving muscles and sinews exposed. Occasionally the pelt would stick in a wound, whereupon he gave it a tug, a clot of dry blood fell to earth, his knife scraped the spot clean and he went on with his work. When he got to the neck, he seemed to do a trick in which he twisted the skin around his left hand, while his right eased the bloody knife under the fur, cut it loose from the eyes and teeth, and with one pull left the rabbit, bereft of its pelt, dangling from a hook, bright red, without tail or ears, its teeth like tiny staves and its front paws hanging limply. Seeing them naked with those gaunt bodies and long legs, Mila suddenly thought they looked like men, men such as had never been seen before, but who even in death felt everything that was occurring and grinned with the mocking, death's-head leer of a tortured criminal. When Anima plunged his knife into their bellies to scrape out the guts, Mila was forced to shut her eyes and an icy shudder pierced her heart, as though the poacher were a cruel executioner whose greatest joy lay in mutilating his innocent fellows. So upon hearing that someone wanted her in the sitting room, she escaped, panting as though she had held her breath all the while, like someone fleeing with troubled conscience from a forbidden place where they did things no decent person would wish to see.

The room had taken on an entirely different aspect. Beneath the wildly ringing bells, whose sound poured from the belfry like a waterfall and crashed in through the wide-open window, the band from Murons was tuning up, while six or seven priests from neighboring villages came and went, shouting, laughing, joking, their somber cassocks interrupting the horns' brassy flash. Everyone was getting ready for St. Pontius' High Mass.

As Mila entered, she heard the rector from Murons telling Gaietà to sound the first call, and after chasing that mob of children from the steeple, he solemnly rang the bells. Mila, who had gone out onto the balcony, saw everyone around her instantly spring into action, like a squadron of ants surprised by a downpour.

Fowls were hastily plucked, camp fires multiplied...and at the last call to Mass, skirts were brushed, bright kerchiefs were tied around heads, voices shouted, feet hurried, and everyone pressed toward the chapel. By the time the rector appeared behind the altar, flanked by priests in liturgical robes adorned with gold and embroidery, the room was packed to bursting. Men, women, and children squeezed together, poked, and cursed each other in whispers as they tried to find a little space to breathe. And since the chapel was too small for so many thousands of worshippers, they filled the yard, stood on steps, sat on walls and even overflowed onto the pine slopes below, stretching their necks to glimpse the ceremony at the altar and holding up bouquets of roses, which they tried to preserve from the crush.

Halfway through the Epistle, a waxy face near the altar suddenly fluttered its eyelids, which closed over dilated pupils, while the head sank against a nearby shoulder... God only knows how they opened a path to carry the woman outside. During the Gospel they had to repeat the procedure with an old man and a child, and by the closing prayers no one in the chapel retained his normal appearance: all their faces were either flushed or white as sheets.

The incense and burning tapers, the heady scent of flowers and the heat from that huddled mass took everyone's breath away. Those bright lights and bobbing red priests around the celebrant dizzied the onlookers, while the racket from the choir, whose voices poured forth and then abruptly halted, the prolonged squeals of the violins, and the coronet's sonorous, echoing tones intoxicated even the most insensitive ears. By the time the service was half over, the crowd had begun to wilt: breasts heaved like bellows, sweat trickled down brows, hearts beat more heavily and muscles grew slack. But refusing to give in, they all stood their ground, awaiting the climactic moment: the blessing that would end the Mass.

At last the ceremony drew to an end, and as the crowd sang Hail Marys and placed a ceremonial cape on the rector's shoulders, half of them eddied and shoved to get out of the chapel, while the other half quietly lined up behind the saint, who had been gently lifted onto four men's shoulders. Then the procession began. The bells' delirious clamor could be heard a mile away. In the courtyard, the church choir swelled into a multitude, and the entire mountain burst into frantic acclamation:

"St. Pontius!"

"St. Pontius!...St. Pontius!...St. Pontius!"

The strange and melancholy saint, even older and shabbier amid that explosion of eternal rebirth, had just become visible outside the doorway's dark rectangle, lifted above the crowded heads, motionless in his gilded cage with its four twisted columns, his slender neck contorted beneath the weight of its miter, holding his crozier in one hand, while the other raised two gnarled fingers and offered the sickly horde his eternal gift of health.

And when that dead and rigid gesture sprang to life and the rector raised his aspergillum, ready to invest those roses with mysterious hidden powers, the crowd, electrified by the sovereign miracle's impenetrable secret, fell silent, humbly knelt, and bowed their heads to earth.

Then Mila, who had returned to the balcony, beheld a black sea of bodies, above which swaying roses seemed to tremble in exalted triumph, as though a divine breeze passed through their midst, reviving and caressing them. That sweet-smelling kingdom absorbed everything except the crowd's senses, which, awakened by the heady spectacle, for a moment rose to ecstatic heights.

Mila too felt the pain of that ecstasy.

She found herself pressed against the balcony railing, her face wet with tears and her heart sweetly shaken by an exquisite turbulence. The earth vanished from before her and Heaven's glory filled her soul.

"St. Pontius!...St. Pontius!...St. Pontius!" The crowd again bellowed, and that shout, wildly repeated and passionately intoned, made her feel for the first time sainthood's great, pure, and lofty empire.

After the first blessing, the procession made its way along the right side of the yard. The human sea parted with difficulty before the tabernacle and then quickly flowed together behind the musicians, whose strident notes clashed with volleys fired by the district's hunters, and beneath a pale noon sky, candles cast white reflections on the worshippers' robes.

When the procession reached the steps in the middle of the yard, the rector again raised his right hand and blessed the roses, all of them, those wilting in bouquets and those opening upon luxuriant bushes.

After presiding over the final benediction of the year, St. Pontius made his way around the yard and, bouncing triumphantly upon those four men's shoulders, returned to his chapel, followed by the throng.

Only one ceremony remained, and while each family sliced its bread and browned its rice, whose aroma would have roused even a dying man's appetite, the hermitage shook with the sound of a thousand vibrant voices:

Sooner than other mortals
You left your mother's womb
To mock cunning Satan
Who lurks beyond the tomb.

And those voices' enthusiasm was echoed even more warmly after each verse by the refrain:

Since God accorded you
Such blessings and wealth,
Give us, oh glorious martyr,
Life and good health.

Then the roses, seeing their festival at an end and resigning themselves to a noble death, drooped and fell to earth, carpeting the mountain with limp petals.

IX. Riot

A pair of long tables mounted on trestles stretched from one end of the sitting room to the other – rented, with cloths and other accoutrements, from a hotel in Murons. The bedroom contained two more, slender and wobbly, while another round one stood below the belfry stairs and still another rested on the well outside, not to mention one in the kitchen, where those from the house or attached to it (Anima, the cooks, and their assistants) hoped to eat, though in fact their intentions were thwarted by the crowd.

By twelve thirty, all those tables – except the round one, which was reserved for the priests – were surrounded by hungry and boisterous throngs.

As soon as the hymns in the chapel ended, those without provisions fell upon the hermitage like a conquering army. They surged through all the rooms, poking, sniffing, and demanding everything. They shouted in the courtyard, swarmed into the kitchen, where they pestered the poor women trying to finish their work, used the corral as a latrine, forced their way into the sheep shed, beat on the cypresses with sticks, invaded the terrace, ripping up handfuls of flowers, spat in the catch basins, climbed the almond trees, from which they shook down the nuts, threw rocks at curious lambs sticking their muzzles through the door to the shed, and like so many fools, left nothing undisturbed.

But as they grew hungrier and wearied of strolling, poking and defiling, they congregated on the upper floor, where they uproariously besieged the dining room.

Some fought over chairs, while others set upon a wobbly table, pulling at its cloth and making the glasses rattle. One, clutching a pencil stub, wrote obscenities on the wall in a childish hand; others clapped and swayed in imitation of a clumsy snake dance... Still others made a circle by the window where, whenever a priest appeared, they would softly begin to chant that song about:

> *A friar and a nun*
> *who slept together...*

which they embellished with winks and nudges, provoking violent blushes in two devout little old ladies swept along by the tide. Another gang of worthy youths in flashy neckties and new caps offered loud wisecracks to the assemblage, at whom they glared as if inviting everyone to applaud their brilliance. As Mila and her assistants passed, they stuck out their legs to trip them, pinched their bottoms, and tickled their armpits. The women shot artfully through their midst like bolts of lightning, bringing salads, arranging places, pouring wine and giving unheeded warnings. Matias also had his work cut out for him. He went from one circle to another, preferably those with the most women, showing off St. Pontius' little shrine lined with velvety paper, the one that had so enraged his wife. After holding forth on its decorations and the saint's glorious miracle, he sold hymns printed on yellow paper in letters as big as grains of millet, pictures on transparent sheets that fluttered in every breeze, brass medals with pictures of the Roquissos in relief, and blessed rosaries and scapulars... If no one wished to buy, he would smilingly request a penny for the saint's festival, unembarrassed when people asked which saint he referred to: the wooden one or another of flesh and blood? Nor was he perturbed by the lewd remarks about his pretty wife. He paid no attention, and when Mila scowled at him in passing, she saw her husband cheerfully going about his business, pocketing pennies as avidly as any gypsy at a fair, while a crowd of children clustered around him, staring or, in the boldest cases, asking for the little chapel. Upon being told no, they writhed and kicked in their mothers' arms, screaming vengefully that they wanted to go home, were sleepy, had a stomach-ache, or...every other imaginable whine.

The lateness of the meal increased the mob's noisy impatience. Some threatened to leave, others clucked in disapproval, till finally the first dish of steaming food appeared in a doorway, held high by a pair of ruddy arms. A great cry went up, chairs were hastily pulled forward, amidst shoves, curses, and yanked up skirts, and the throng tumbled over each other like figs in a basket. In a flash, the tables were surrounded by two circles as tightly packed as two soldered iron rings. But the dish crossed the room, leaving a tantalising aroma in its wake, and entered the door to the belfry. It was for the priests.

As it dawned on the crowd that the clergy would be served first, a murmur of protest arose, a kind of electric current activating the dormant anticlericalism in their souls, a secret rage, a wave of bitter impotence that quickly led to dirty looks and angry threats.

And when the dishes were finally placed on those long tables and there was abundant food for one and all, that wrath, as though peppering palates and heating blood to a boil, quickly filled their brains with spiteful red smoke.

The rings were broken and resoldered by those who came and went, the former having waited for a place and the latter having eaten hastily, but the number seated remained the same and the meal went on and on. The smacking of lips, the gurgle of those who drank in jets from wineskins, the tinkle of glasses and cutlery mingled with the sounds of conversation and laughter, filling the rooms, whose air grew thick with the stench of charred meat, foul breath, wine, belches, and pestilent clouds of tobacco smoke. Even before beginning, the meal had taken on a disordered Saturnalian air. The men's eyes sparkled, their greasy lips parted as they smiled from ear to ear, their eager hands reached out to fondle whatever flesh was within reach, and their ribald comments fell on ears like stones upon a rooftop.

The single women, or those with friends but without men at their sides, beat a hasty retreat, followed by families tagging behind disgruntled fathers and brothers, and the priests, whose flushed faces cautiously appeared in the doorway and who, alarmed by the commotion, quietly slipped down the stairs to the chapel.

Then the shepherd, who had been observing the scene for a while, stopped Mila at the door and said: "Keep out of there, hermitess. The place is worse than a kennel... Remember what I told you the other day? They're so drunk they can't walk and they're spoiling for a fight... In a little while we'll have to shoo them out with a broom."

Without objecting, Mila returned to the kitchen, where other uninvited guests were still gorging away, while the vulgar bacchanal continued under Gaietà's troubled and scornful gaze, which fell upon those so-called higher animals who bellowed and seethed, drunk on high spirits, ill-digested food, proximity and a little wine: everything that might inebriate a so-called lower species.

Outside in the sunshine, all was serene. Laughter echoed melodiously, red faces beamed beneath a clear blue sky, limbs, with easeful lassitude, adopted classical poses, unpleasant smells dissipated in the open air, while pleasant ones hung suspended like aromatic caresses. Wineglasses in uplifted hands glittered like opals or garnets, knives gleamed as they cut into ripe fruit, and satisfied bellies, engendering wit and wisdom, inspired a flow of clever anecdotes and fairy tales.

In each clearing, a family made the most of its holiday, free of superfluous members: the idle, the unmarried, all the components of that vipers' nest above, caged in the hermitage where they roared their satisfaction with the afternoon's pleasures.

The kings of those clearings were the children, who frolicked and squealed, eating till they nearly burst, running their greasy fingers over their mothers' faces, squirming and chattering. Nearby, horses and donkeys, still hitched to their carts, looked up pensively from their feedbags, with wisps of alfalfa or straw on their lips, and watched the excitement from big dark eyes full of inexpressible thoughts. Then, with philosophic indifference, they returned to their meal, chewing and switching their tails, while their masters let loose an entire winter's pent-up energies beneath the brilliant May sun.

Profiting from the crowd's sense of well-fed contentment, vendors picked their way among them: a one-eyed Castilian with a box of watch chains, sets of cheap buttons, suspenders, pencils, and wallets, an old lady selling hazelnuts, her face red and wrinkled as a withered apple and her body bent under a heavy wicker basket of rattling wares, the men selling packets of star anise and sweets, half-melted in their fly-specked wrappers, the orange vendor, holding a golden orb aloft and crying: "Sweet and juicy, girls!", a shopkeeper from Murons with bottles of lemonade and soda... All seductive, insinuating, free with honeyed words and tempting offers that roused an irresistible and contagious wish to buy...

Parents and grandparents, yielding to insistent young voices, purchased gooey treats and laughed to see them popped into children's mouths. The vainer adolescents reluctantly searched their pockets before bringing forth the coins to buy those blue buttons that would go so well with that mauve shirt. An enamored fiancé, beholding the premature gleam in his beloved's eyes, filled her lap with oranges and in return asked to suck a little where she had bitten.

Meanwhile, in nearby fields and hollows, beneath the resinous scent of umbrella pines, and in the shadows of wagons as immobile as gun carriages on a battlefield, men in shirtsleeves, stupefied by their feast, either stretched out near their wives, who gently sang lullabies to the infants in their laps, or lay within sight of some marriageable young thing who looked back submissively from time to time, as a serf might gaze upon her lord and master.

Behind a wall, strong arms encircled a soft, yielding body, while further off a couple gazed at each other lovingly, and still further, hidden behind a rise, a head lay against a shoulder and lips met with fierce desire.

In that glutted stillness, the race's reproductive instincts, aroused and almost uncontrollable, eluded chaperons' sleepy eyes and followed their course...till the band struck up the first *sardana*.

Seated on the walls at each side of the chapel door or leaning against them, the musicians, with rigid bodies and contorted faces, looked like a row of gargoyles. They solemnly performed a comic pantomime, raising and lowering eyebrows, rolling eyes, puffing out cheeks, while those metal extensions of their lips rained cascades of notes upon the crowd, magically rousing men and women and calling them forth to dance.

And, like ripples from a drop in a still pond, the throng quickly formed circles and more circles, perfectly concentric, that shifted right and left, weaving their sacred steps rhythmically, mathematically, till the nearby pine groves were empty except for an occasional couple, who remained hand in hand, their eyes fixed upon each other. The house also emptied at the first breath of music, and only a few women lingered to struggle with the dirty dishes or kneel before the chapel's altars, fervently reciting prayers learnt by heart to the saint of their devotion, while a handful of eccentrics, who disliked all the commotion and who held their berets in hands clasped behind their backs, wandered about scrutinizing the votive offerings and quietly sounding out their monotonous inscriptions.

The sun, making its way westward across the clear blue sky, showered the multitude with golden rays that glittered on the Civil Guards' shiny black hats and the musicians' silver instruments.

Suddenly, no one knew how or why, a cry rang out, followed by a slap and a few terrified screams, whereupon in that same corner of the yard, sticks were hastily raised and the crowd grew thicker.

"What's going on?"

"What is it?" a few frightened voices asked.

"Someone threw a punch," others replied, while the brawl quickly spread toward the center of the dance.

The outer circles were broken first, followed by the others, and in the middle of the packed mob, a knife flashed and shots were fired.

An infernal cry arose, a sort of unanimous bellow, dominated by women's screams and sobs, while the musicians, pale as ghosts, their eyes frozen in their sockets, hadn't the wit to lay down the instruments they had abruptly silenced.

"Break it up!" cried the pair of Civil Guards, pushing through the crowd. When they reached the center of the fray, they repeated their command. No one paid any attention. A heap of men clutched each other and brayed, spitting out curses and insults, while others tried to separate them and women screamed in each others' arms.

"Cut it out, *brutos!*" the sergeant cried again in Castilian. "Break it up or I'll..."

And fulfilling his threat, he aimed his rifle butt at one of the ringleaders' heads. But then something strange happened. The brawling stopped and everyone turned to face the two guards. There was a moment's hesitation, as when a bull is about to charge, and then a clear and vibrant voice shouted: "Go to Hell!"

The entire crowd sprang into action.

"Go to Hell!"

"Go to Hell!"

"Go to Hell!" cried twenty-five voices in simultaneous protest.

The sergeant pulled himself up and glared angrily around him.

"Break it up, I said, or there's going to be trouble!"

Another instigator stepped forth from the mass, while the others stood up, encouraged by the mob's support, and glowered back.

One insult led to another, the sergeant lost patience and shouldered his weapon while his partner imitated him, and the entire yard erupted. The furious crowd took the rebels' side and curses rained down upon the pair, isolated amidst the tumult. Wine and liquor had performed their civilizing mission, heating tempers and loosening tongues. At the sight of that gathering storm, mules and donkeys were quickly hitched, while families, vendors and other peaceable folk, hoisting bundles and stuffing leftovers into bags, hurried down the mountainside as fast as their legs could carry them. The paths and trails were filled with clamor and terrified voices.

"They stood up to the guards..."

"I heard someone was shot..."

"And ten wounded..."

"The sergeant was hopping mad..."

"But who started it all?"

No one was certain, but they slowly pieced the story together.

Marbles, Lefty, Catear and Strawberry, the prides of their respective parishes (Llisquents, Ridorta, Murons, and Roquesalbes), all of whom drunkenly recalled old rivalries, had bet on who could dance the best *sardana*. Each one, declaring himself champion of his village, politely danced the first number with his gang of followers. Once it was over, disputes arose over who had won. Then the second dance began, but as no one knew which way to move, some went left and some right, while the calmer souls stopped to complain and the more exalted ones declared their champions victorious. The calmer ones' serenity, however, went up in smoke with the first blow, and from then on the brawl had gone as predictably as clockwork.

The results: with help from all the authorities and policemen at the gathering, the pair of Civil Guards managed to subdue the most intrepid rioters and place them under arrest. Those who had also gotten out of hand but had no wish to face the consequences disappeared into what remained of the crowd: some hundred men who, still aroused, milled about uncertainly and at last followed the guards and prisoners down the hill.

By evening, the only visitor left was that poor hazelnut seller, who sat moaning in the kitchen, her head wrapped in a bandage, while tears trickled down her withered apple of a face. Somehow she had been caught in the middle of the fray and, tossed from one group to another, had been shoved through the gate and down the steps outside.

Matias had found her afterward, dazed, with a cut ear and a dislocated arm. The old woman, between groans and sobs, was still thanking blessed St. Pontius for preserving her, at her eighty-odd years, from broken bones.

Baldiret stood nearby, impatiently waiting for Mila and

Gaietà to finish cleansing the woman's cuts and bruises with wine, and upon seeing the shepherd wash his hands at the sink, the boy rubbed his head against his shoulder and tugged at the shepherd's sleeve.

"What is it, son?"

"How about those lights?"

"God Almighty! This is a fine time for lanterns!" exclaimed Mila, remembering everything that had occurred. But Gaietà wiped his hands and smiled affectionately at the boy.

"Wait a second! That's not such a bad idea! A little light's just what we need after such a gloomy afternoon. Why should those swine have all the fun?" And clapping his hands, he cried: "All right, let's get the oil!"

And while shadows streaked the earth, as from a passing flock of ravens, Gaietà and his friend filled the snail shells they had nailed to doors, balconies, and windows the day before. An hour later, diminutive lamps glowed in the mountains' high solitude, where the scent of violence still seemed to linger, and outlined the hermitage with tiny points of light, making it look like a fairy palace in one of Gaietà's stories.

X. Relics

Next morning, Gaietà found the front gates unbolted and went out to see who had risen so early. As he looked down the slope, he spied Mila seated on a boulder, her arms dangling limply, staring into the distance.

"What got you up so early, hermitess? You're just like a child..."

Mila slowly turned to face the shepherd. Her gaze was as blank and desolate as the day he'd shown her the belfry, and her pale, expressionless face resembled a marble head with painted lips. Gaietà was surprised. She tried to climb down, but her steps were unsteady, as though her legs had been hobbled by an invisible rope. The shepherd reached up to help her.

"You aren't sick, are you?" he asked uneasily.

As swiftly and unexpectedly as a falcon seizes its prey, she clasped his wrinkled hand in her soft fingers, pulling him toward her.

"Look!" she mumbled hoarsely, like one who has just awakened. And she pointed to several places in the hollow below them. Though Gaietà then understood the cause of her mood, he lacked the courage to reply. She again stared into the distance and nervously bit her lip. When the shepherd tired to free his hand, she clasped it more tightly.

"Oh! And don't think that's all!" Still holding his hand, she rushed down the rocky slope, while the shepherd struggled to keep up with her, and led him to the fig trees, the orchard, the Roar, the pine groves... Each time they stopped, she bit her lip harder and her eyes grew colder till at last Gaietà, placing his other hand upon hers, halted that overheated machine by crying: "Now stop that! Don't show me any more! I knew about it before you did!"

"Did you ever see anything so sad?" she replied, holding back her tears.

The man shrugged his shoulders.

"What can you do, hermitess?... For years I've thought folks aren't as good as they should be, but it's no use banging your head against the wall. That won't solve anything... God'll help those who need Him, y'know?"

"They broke all my pots!"

"Well, good thing it wasn't your ribs instead... Ask that old hazelnut lady..."

He tried to smile bravely, but her expression stopped him.

"And they didn't even pay for it!"

"Listen: don't think I'm saying I told you so, but remember what I said the day before yesterday? I warned you not to trust anyone with as much as a clove of garlic. You're too nice and don't look people over close enough. Someone who's emptyhanded: say goodbye and good luck to him! I didn't let anyone out of the sitting room without paying..."

"They all said they'd pay when they brought the stuff back, and here's the thanks I get."

"Hermitess, sometimes you act like a babe in arms. Stuff you don't get paid for in advance is stuff you can kiss goodbye. Once they've eaten their fill, they'll cram what's left into their sacks. And if they don't have sacks they'll smash your casseroles, use your pitchers for target practice, throw your silverware in the bushes, and without wasting a cent they've cleaned up their mess!"

"I thought people got scared by that brawl and tried to escape, but that afterward they'd come back one by one, and I'd find all my stuff scattered around, but when I saw everything broken..." Mila replied, humiliated.

The shepherd smiled pityingly.

"I could see that's what you were thinking and I didn't want to argue, but I was afraid it would turn out like this... Well, you'll just have to get over it. And you might as well forget about what they owe you... Just imagine everyone paid and then some thief stole your strongbox."

Mila felt a lump in her throat.

"There's something you don't know: Matias spent everything we had on that festival..."

Gaietà looked up in alarm.

"How's that?"

"The house was empty, remember? We bought everything ourselves... He said we'd make a fortune...and the rector, and the people at St. Pontius all said the same. We spent two weeks stocking up on food and pots...till we were broke... You saw us..."

"Sure I did, hermitess, and I was worried..."

He fell silent for a moment and then shyly asked: "So now what're you going to do?"

Mila stared straight at him, her green eyes filled with the mysterious calm of a deep gorge.

"Now? Now that we've lost my uncle's house and all our savings, if they don't pay us we'll have to stay here, poorer and nakeder than Adam and Eve."

And feeling a savage tug at her heart, she added dully: "These are the relics old St. Pontius left us!"

The bitterness behind her words made her hardened face seem older.

Gaietà looked at her and thought: "This lady's going to worry herself to death. If she doesn't snap out of it, there'll be trouble ahead..." He glanced at her eyes, which were cold and dry as flint.

They surveyed the mountain, which was like an abandoned battlefield: broken pots and smashed glassware, one piece in a hundred still whole, an occasional cup, fork, or plate that she gathered up, gritting her teeth, for such remains only heightened her fury. In one spot, hidden by weeds, they saw a handkerchief with a knotted corner, and inside that knot, which Gaietà carefully untied, a couple of pennies.

"Look here, hermitess... Some girl must have been fixing to bury her savings."

The kind shepherd tried to make Mila laugh, but her brow remained furrowed.

They also found an espadrille, a new jug, a dirty napkin tossed behind some blackberry bushes, a pocket knife amid all the refuse: greasy paper, orange peels, squashed roses, well-gnawed spare ribs, bits of chicken covered with black ants, dead campfires...all the festival's repulsive debris.

On their return home, they met Matias, who had just risen and was still stretching and yawning, his eyes narrow, his face puffy, and in no mood to talk. As soon as he spied them at the kitchen door, he dropped onto the bench like a sullen child, rubbing his eyes and grumbling: "Well, where've you been? What happened to my breakfast?"

Mila was stunned for a moment by that surly greeting. Then she suddenly felt the blood rush to her head like a pistol shot. Her lip trembled, her eyes flashed like a cat's, her forehead broke out in red blotches... She approached her husband with the swift movement of an attacking beast.

"You want your breakfast...eh? Your break...fast? Go outside... You'll find your breakfast...there!"

She could say no more. Her words came forth slowly, like beads on a rosary, one by one, with deep breaths between them.

It was the first time Gaietà had seen her in such a temper.

Matias, who had miraculously awakened with a jolt, now looked at her as though about to flee, his eyes wide and astonished.

Hoping to give Mila a chance to recover, the shepherd hastily explained everything to Matias, who was then even more astounded. Resting his elbows on the table and with a glazed look in his eyes, he spent five puzzled minutes rubbing a crack in the wood. Then he began a series of useless questions, idle suppositions, empty threats...

Mila gazed at him with the scornful fury she always felt for his spinelessness, and unconsciously, above his lowered eyes, her own sought refuge in the shepherd's. He stared back at her, and those eyes full of strength, foresight, and serenity enveloped her in a broad, warm, devoted, infinite gaze...

Mila felt a sudden explosion in her chest, and the ground gave way beneath her. Darkness fell, as though a lightning bolt...

At that moment Baldiret shouted from outside: "My brother's here! My brother's here!"

And indeed, Arnau soon entered the kitchen with a whip slung around his neck, his trousers cuffed at the ankles, and a straw hat shading his tanned face. A breath of youthful vigor seemed to enter with him.

The shepherd and Matias greeted their guest affectionately, while Mila stood silently against the wall as though she had never met him.

Arnau had brought the wagon to collect everything rented from the hotel and cart it back to Murons.

They all sat down to breakfast, during which they spoke of nothing but the past day's quarrels and breakages...till Arnau said: "We had our share too! They stole my mom's rabbits..."

"What? Your mother's rabbits?"

"And they hit the farm below us too...looks like there's

a mighty smart greyhound sniffing around these hills!"

Everyone read a particular name into Arnau's words: one that had occurred to all of them simultaneously. Mila began to fret, and as soon as the meal was over and the men were loading the wagon with tables and silverware, she went out to the yard by the sheep shed. She had been so anxious about her pots and dishes that she had thrown a skirtful of food into a corner without looking around. Most of it was still lying there. Only two pregnant rabbits, round as balls, twitched their long, ashy ears among the leaves. She looked everywhere; the others were nowhere to be seen. She smiled bitterly. Her morning rage had disappeared, reduced to a cold depression through which she viewed each new setback.

When the wagon was loaded, Gaietà left and Matias went to wash up before going to settle their accounts. Mila then called Arnau and showed him the empty yard.

"Well, what did you expect? Yours were the closest to hand!" He laughed. "I bet they escaped!"

And since Mila didn't understand, he searched the yard till he found a hole that had been scratched behind a rock.

"Look!... Didn't I tell you?" And poking the handle of his whip through the opening, he insisted: "There, that's how they got away...just like at our place. So no one can say they were stolen... The bastard!"

"So that's where he got all those rabbits!" exclaimed Mila. "I couldn't believe he'd trapped them all...but why did he make those holes if everyone knows it's him?"

"He doesn't care what people think, as long as they can't prove anything."

Arnau's mouth twisted into a contemptuous sneer. Mila noticed his lips, full and red like an exotic fruit. The bright enamel of his teeth and the brown line of his growing mustache set them off, making them his most prominent feature.

Leaping from one thought to another, Mila suddenly asked: "Well, when's your wedding, Arnau?"

"I'm not getting married," he mumbled.

"What do you mean, you're not getting married?" she asked, laughing.

"I said I'm not getting married," Arnau replied, toying with the whip and staring at the ground.

"I know it's not right away, but..."

"Not right away or ever," he quickly replied.

Mila was amazed.

"Come on! You're joking!...I saw you with her yesterday!"

"Well, you won't see us together again..."

"Mother of God! Why not?"

Arnau hesitated, blushed, and slowly mumbled: "We broke up..."

Mila stared at him in disbelief.

"What do you mean?"

But seeing his crestfallen look, she gently added: "What happened, Arnau?"

Arnau, embarrassed, unwound the whip from his fingers, rewound it, and finally blurted out, with a shrug of his shoulders: "Tsk! You know how it is..."

Mila curiously looked him up and down.

Standing before her straight and tall, he breathed power and good health. Though not exactly handsome, he had the seductive charm of youth. Finding nothing else to say and remembering how pleased his family had been with the match, Mila wondered: "Why would she leave this poor fellow?" And her mute question was followed by another spoken though indirect one.

"Well, I can hardly believe my ears... I thought it was all set and we'd be cutting the cake soon."

"Sometimes people change their minds...they think one thing and then another..."

Arnau took the whip from around his neck and began

poking the ground with its handle.

"Everyone said she was crazy about you!"

"She was."

"And so were you..."

The lad hung his head even lower and prodded the ground with renewed energy.

"Maybe...before," he finally replied.

Mila was even more perplexed.

"So now you're not interested? God Almighty!... What did she do?"

Arnau quickly raised his head and snapped back: "She didn't do anything! It was my fault..."

His words only piqued Mila's curiosity further, and she replied: "Come on! That doesn't make sense! She didn't do anything, it's your fault, and you still broke up with her?"

Mila smiled.

Arnau glanced back at her, raised his whip, and cracked it fiercely, sending the two pregnant rabbits scurrying across the yard.

Since he refused to respond, Mila continued to play innocent and hotly declared: "Sometimes I wonder what you men have in mind!..."

Arnau raised his head and seemed to reach a swift decision.

"You want to know why? I left her because you can't love two girls at once, and it's not right to lead people on..."

Mila stopped in her tracks.

"Ah!... So you mean..."

"You know that song: *I don't love the one they gave me. The one I love...?*" He interrupted himself, and bravely looking her in the eye, added in another tone: "If only she knew how much I love her!"

Mila received another shock, this time of mingled fear and sorrow, though not surprise. And at the same time she realized that, without having put it into so many words, she already knew that Arnau had been in love with her for some time, that she had guessed the unspoken purpose of his frequent visits to the hermitage, the hidden meaning of those admiring glances. Caution and shame had veiled them in the past, but now, unnerved by that morning's fierce and restless tides, Mila had carelessly rent the veil, through which the glances shot straight at her, demanding a categorical reply to the declaration she had solicited.

Arnau, standing tall, bathed in sunlight and strong as a young fir, was only two steps away. Mila felt afraid of those penetrating eyes that burned with desire, of those provocative lips, red and voluptuous, of that torso bursting with masculine power, of the heady waves of passion that swept over her lonely, forgotten life.

She instinctively stepped back lest something irrevocable occur.

Arnau, whose fervent gaze never left her, saw the woman hesitate, blush, and then turn white as a sheet. Trembling, he stepped forward as she recoiled.

They stood there, taking each other's measure like two enemy soldiers overcome by common humanity and a longing to embrace. But it only lasted a second; something suddenly came between them.

Distant eyes, unframed by any face, enveloped the pale woman in a broad, warm, devoted, infinite gaze. And those eyes, as though embodying a force stronger than life itself, made the turbulent wave quickly recede into the distance. Mila regained her composure.

She wiped her brow with one hand and extended the other to Arnau.

"Arnau, don't be childish. If that girl still loves you and you want some good advice, marry her... You might not be so lucky next time."

Arnau heard the reproach, the irrevocable command in

those friendly words. He took the blow unflinchingly and then hung his head, unprotesting. But the shock of pain suffused his face so clearly that Mila could scarcely bear to look at him.

"Arnau," she said gently: "they say a proverb's as good as a song, and you know that one about *a bird in the hand*..."

The boy made a despairing gesture and, slinging the whip around his neck, left without looking back.

Mila watched him recede and felt, with inexplicable grief, that she had just killed something in that innocent and in herself.

XI. Cabin Fever

All summer a stream of visitors made their way up to the hermitage, rescuing Mila from what would otherwise have been a cruel or languid season.

Sometimes they were hunting parties from Barcelona, wearing new hats, weighed down by luxurious gear, their bodies crisscrossed by rifle slings, leading packs of sleek purebred dogs whose rolls of fat shook as they ran. Men and beasts charged about, laughing, barking, and filling the air with stray shots to the dismay of more seasoned hunters. Though only by miracle did those model sportsmen occasionally catch something, they descended upon the house like a ravenous hurricane. There were never enough eggs for all the omelettes they ordered, nor could Mila kill and cook chickens fast enough to satisfy them. And while each ate enough for four, she watched them having the time of their lives, admiring their handsome outfits and bellicose airs, bragging about their exploits with an eloquence that would have done Cyrano de Bergerac credit. She enjoyed observing those mischievous kids playing hooky, and in her mind she compared them to the local hunters, who returned with one pantleg hanging down and another rolled up above their knees, cartridge belts tied with rope, and worn-out espadrilles, but with blood-stained pouches and the muzzles of their weapons ragged as lace from years of spitting so much lethal fire.

Other parties were more peaceful and moderate: devout families who, with their parish priests, came to celebrate Mass at the hermitage in fulfillment of some desperate and hasty vow. Those groups, once the service ended, also laughed and made merry, but with a different sort of merriment, calmer and more pleasant than the hunters'.

Mournful groups also appeared, though infrequently, on Roquís Mitjà's wooded slopes. Mila recalled one that started up the trail toward the end of August. It was led by a dapper old gentleman with a neatly trimmed mustache, followed by a half-dozen people clustered around a horse, on which a misshapen boy rode side-saddle like a woman: a teenager yellow as wax, stiff-necked, his mouth twisted by a chronic abscess. The young man's hand was held, when the path permitted, by a still young and beautiful lady whose eyes, however, were already blank and weary as an old woman's.

Once Mila had welcomed them outside the chapel, the dull-eyed lady explained the reason for their pilgrimage. It was a case of scrofula, and the poor lad, tired of doctors' remedies and despairing of human cures, still retained a vague faith in saints and their miracles. He wanted to bathe in the Roar's waters: those waters so many claimed would purge him of evil humors and cleanse his diseased blood.

And while he rested, shivering with cold in the hottest part of summer, Mila, alone with the servants, learned that the rich lady was a widow with no other relatives than this deformed son, who had been rotten with disease almost from the day of his birth. Together they wandered from town to town, seeking not a cure, of which they had long since abandoned hope, but some improvement, a slight extension of that painful semblance of life, prolonging the tragic immensity of his torment and sacrifice.

And when she helped them bathe the sick boy, when she beheld the true misery of that poor shriveled body covered with lumps and sores, displaying its nakedness to one and all with the shameless indifference of the very ill, Mila suspected for the first time that motherhood, that unquenchable and dreamed-of source of joy and comfort, could sometimes be a punishment for one's sins in other lives.

Except for those cheerful or gloomy visitors, who always brought distraction and a little money, Mila was alone, spending her mornings around the house and her afternoons either in the garden or sewing in some shady spot. Baldiret and Gaietà pastured their flock in the mountains, and Matias headed for the plain, where he made the rounds of all the villages.

St. Pontius' festival had left them utterly destitute. In addition to their losses, Mila learned of infinite debts slowly revealed by Matias: debts for things borrowed from the hotel in Murons, debts in stores and taverns for food and drink he had obtained on credit, debts to the rector for hymns and pictures printed in Girona: a swarm of petty debts that buzzed and bit like mosquitoes and that, as Mila learned of them, provoked endless fear and anxiety. She dreamt of nothing but those debts and how they might pay them, and thus she swallowed her shame about Matias' begging and even agreed to use the proceeds.

"With a little luck, we'll get back on our feet again, and then I'll pay it all back, every last cent..." she told herself each day to ease her conscience, but her face fell whenever Matias returned from his wanderings, showed her his pouch, and suggested how they might spend the money. She wanted to clap her hand over his mouth, make him feel the infamy of his deeds, and at all costs keep the shepherd from learning of their disgrace and condemning them. But Matias understood nothing, and Gaietà listened and judged. His judgment was silent, a judgment she knew he would never reveal in word or deed, but no less severe and implacable for all that. And she who, without realizing it, would have liked to wear a halo in that man's eyes, saw furiously and despairingly that his judgment damned her, placing her on a lower level than bandits, for bandits risked their lives to rob men, whereas she and Matias stole from the very saints at no risk to themselves.

But that desired stroke of luck, which never materialized, seemed to grow more distant with each passing day, while her burden of shame and worry only grew heavier. As autumn approached, the visitors stopped coming, and with them went the better part of her earnings. In September, when the sun still warmed the meadows at midday but cold winds had begun to chill the shadows, only a few solitary strollers from nearby villages, an occasional hunter who asked for a shot of whisky, or, once in a while, a well-to-do gentleman and his wife, who bore a candle in one hand and a picnic basket in the other, climbed the mountain to that isolated hermitage.

The hunters paid for their drinks, and the others, after making her show them everything and wearying her with silly questions, threw a few cents in the poor box, gave her a few more, and congratulated themselves on their splendid generosity.

Finally, even these stopped coming, and with a shiver of fear Mila watched winter sweep down upon the barren mountain, threatening the poor hermitage with its empty larder, its breadless oven, and its ill-suited inhabitants.

Then the woman's placid disposition began to crack, and her black, bitter moods rained down on Matias, normally the world's calmest and most Devil-may-care fellow, poisoning his good humor and making him uneasy. She was always after him, nagging, scolding, literally shoving him out the door in search of a little cash, while he, both annoyed and cowed by that constant pressure, kept yielding till at last he obeyed her almost blindly. He leapt up at the crack of dawn, and with the little shrine on his back, began his long journey down to the plain. The results of this unwonted activity were soon apparent: his lazy fat melted away, the folds on his neck disappeared, his shoulder blades again were visible, the dimples that had made his hands like an abbess' vanished, and the rope that held up his trousers no longer left a red mark around his waist. Even his movements quickened, and his face became alert like other men's.

Mila would have thanked God for these improvements, had they been accompanied by others more financially beneficial, but while Matias' obedient zeal waxed, his earnings waned.

"May God punish us for our sins," the woman repeated bitterly after each fruitless trip, yet the memory of their debts and the pressing need to pay them made her close her eyes to everything and goad him all the more.

Till one evening the shepherd, seeing Matias return after dark, gently rebuked him: "Hermit, this joke's gone far enough! These hills are full of bandits who can smell your money a mile away... I know you don't have much, but you shouldn't let them see you out this late."

Matias said he wasn't afraid and that if he hoped to make something, he had to venture further each day.

Mila also thought Gaietà had nothing to fear, but all the same she decided to nag Matias less.

Shortly thereafter, he stayed out all night, and the next day explained that he had wandered too far afield and Anima had given him shelter.

The shepherd glanced at him suspiciously, and when Matias went to put his shrine down in the sitting room, the old man mumbled: "Maybe I should have kept my mouth shut the other day... Sometimes the cure can be worse than the disease."

"Why?" asked Mila in surprise.

"What can I say? With Anima around..."

Mila smiled at his fears. She was used to the feud between those two, but she couldn't understand why someone so wise and serene would pay so much attention to a savage beast like Anima.

Matias came back, and she thought to herself: "Well, let him poach rabbits, but as for hurting anyone...he's too scared of the police."

And neither then nor all the other times he failed to return did she dare to scold him for staying with Anima, lest he use her words as an excuse to stop begging. But after a few more weeks, his two- and three-day trips became so frequent that the woman began to worry, thinking it was time to clip his wings a little. Matias seemed taken aback by her first warnings and, in the confused, broken words he usually employed, he vaguely promised to improve: "Well, yes... Well, good... I'll see to it... Fine..." And that was all. He continued to behave just as before. Mila then went from warnings to lectures and from lectures to orders, but the effect was always the same: he seemed to yield, but in fact he resisted passively like a reed in the wind, righting himself as soon as the tempest had passed. He set out earlier and earlier, and when she made him promise to return before dusk, he readily agreed, but at dusk he was still absent, and often the following day as well. It was useless to try to detain him with chores around the house. He slipped away like an eel, and when she looked for him he was gone. His lethargy seemed to have vanished with his fat, and she found him swift as a chamois and cunning as a fox. She had to admit that the change was greater than she had supposed, that something or other had been stronger than herself, that some new element had entered his life, toppling those walls of dull indifference and estranging the two of them even more than before.

The woman raged against this new defeat, and at night in their empty bed, she lay on her stomach biting the damp, cool pillowcase.

And to make her rout more complete, she noticed that the more he stayed away, the poorer he returned and the more eager to leave again. Finally she asked the shepherd's opinion, and he replied: "I try not to think the worst of people, and it's kind of hard to say...but anyhow, I don't think your husband's begging like he says... The other day I was up near Roepass when all of a sudden I spotted two specks in the distance, beyond Olivebreath, near Wild Goat Falls. They were too little to make out, but I'd have sworn it was him and Anima... Olivebreath's not on the way to town, and it's no use asking the birds for charity. So they couldn't have been begging. I reckon the other one took him along to trap rabbits, and your husband's the kind...that doesn't like to argue. But don't say anything till I know for sure. I'll keep an eye out...all right?"

Mila kept quiet, but her spirits sagged beneath the weight of this new trial, and her loneliness deepened, freezing her soul like a glacier. October ended and the sunsets came earlier and earlier, trimming the brief days with shadowy scissors. Matias spent only two nights a week at the hermitage. Arnau hadn't visited her since that encounter in the yard, and Anima had disappeared after St. Pontius' festival. The mountains seemed empty except for those women from Ridorta, always bent beneath their bundles of firewood, nor did Gaietà return for a midday nap as he once had, but kept his flock out at pasture from ten to four every day. Then, instead of settling himself in the kitchen, he took Baldiret's hand and led him to Murons, where the boy could receive an hour's instruction till the winter came, at which time he would return home and spend all day in the classroom. Gaietà hoped thus to prepare Mila for the shock of losing him, but it did her little good. Alone in the house, waiting endlessly in that dark, deserted kitchen, without real tasks to occupy her idle hours, she felt a deep and painful sadness steal over her. That morning she had given Gaietà and Baldiret their lunch. Her own was simmering on the fire, and free of all necessity or desire to act, she pressed against the kitchen window that looked out on Roquís Mitjà or leaned on the railing around the terrace that faced east. Then she saw the flock set out, preceded by Baldiret's cries, guided by Mussol's barks, and followed by the shepherd with a sheepskin pouch slung across his dark wool jacket, his cap pulled down and a cape over his shoulders, holding out his crook, stamping his heavy shoes solemnly and slowly, but without the slightest trace of laziness or exhaustion.

The grazing sheep spread across the mountain, covering its black, wet earth like a shifting patch of snow. Baldiret ran here and there, turning after each leap to smile back at Mila and call out his goodbyes, while the man also usually turned a few times and waved to her with his staff...till that patch of snow disappeared in the distance, insubstantial as a cloud of dust, and Mila remained at her lookout with glistening eyes, standing there till two tears fell upon her crossed arms. Others soon followed in silver rivulets down her cheeks, and finally she burst into sobs, at first timid and tremulous as a new-born babe's, then more urgent and unrestrained, and in the end wild howls of pain, boredom, and longing that went on and on as though emptying a stream in which she was drowning. When they stopped, dying away slowly amid moans and sniffles, she was left exhausted, with swollen lids and a great lead weight behind her eyes. Then, weary and listless, she wandered through the house and fields, staring dully at the sad, whitewashed walls, the clear blue sky, the crisply outlined mountains that were now turning brown. Pacing like a soul in torment, she seemed to await something uncertain, something disturbing that should have come yet never materialized. Then even her desire to walk vanished, leaving her dozing for hours upon her bed, or sitting at the table with her back to the light.

Her decline was swift: she stopped eating and grew pale and bony, while her gaze was as blank and weary as that rich widowed mother's. She lost her taste for everything, including neatness, and went about with crooked skirts and runs in her stockings. She let holes appear at the elbows of Matias' jacket, while those in his trouser pockets grew larger.

Gaietà was alarmed by the woman's state.

"Hermitess!" he cried one day when he found her weeping and she had to admit she didn't know why. "You've been sick for a while and we'd better find some medicine, but not the kind you can get from a doctor... You're not happy up here, and the only cure is to have some fun, though it's true there's not much to do in these parts. First of all, you can't stay here like a bat in a cave. No one can live without company, y'know? Tomorrow we'll lock the hermitage and you'll come with us. Not a soul ever visits you except your husband, and if he finds you gone, he can wait or go back where he came from. He's not much use to anyone now..."

And sweetening his solemn words with a smile, he announced, without consulting Mila, that she would accompany him the next day: "You'll see it's not so bad...and if you don't feel like waiting, ask the boy."

Mila meekly acquiesced, as though her will had been taken from her, and tagged along behind the flock like an obedient child. Gaietà entertained her with his stories, they stopped to eat beneath the Husk, she watched Baldiret shoot his slingshot and later helped him study his ABCs from a primer the shepherd carried in his bag...

As they descended Roquís Mitjà's whale-like back, while the sheep played tag around them on their way to the hermitage, she realized with amazement that for the first time in many days she hadn't counted the hours. A cool and pleasant breeze, announcing the evening, seemed to dissipate her torpor and rouse her sleeping energies.

XII. Time Past

Autumn had come, bringing with it cold weather. One gray day followed another, and the distant mountains were so shrouded in fog that not a ray of sunlight or sharp outline disturbed their chaste poetry. Everything seemed gentle and hazy as a dream, inviting spirits to soften their rough edges.

Through these misty landscapes, like animated figures in an enormous painting, Mila wandered with her friends, who kept watch over her virginal and perplexed convalescence.

Slowly but surely, she began to recover, and her reawakening brought many a joyful surprise. As though some divine hand had plucked the sting from her troubles, they no longer pierced her as before but buzzed harmlessly about her head, nor was the hermitage a jail but a haven, a nest where, like a bird, she rested between flights.

Those harsh and deserted mountains, full of majestic vistas seen from uncharted trails chosen by whim and fancy, became a setting for peaceful hours of enjoyment. She now viewed Matias, her former companion, from the serene heights of benevolent indifference. She scolded him no more and troubled neither him nor herself, as though the violent tie through which she once hoped to bind him had now broken noiselessly and painlessly, leaving their lives forever sundered, and with that unspoken divorce, all the tensions between their natures seemed to vanish. She felt free to act as she liked, and with this secret liberty, harmony reigned in her thoughts and deeds. Though it was a dull harmony, devoid of strength and vibrancy, for this very reason it pleased the woman, from whom it demanded little effort.

Like a soldier who has lost blood on the battlefield and must regain it drop by drop, Mila slowly revived. But if a dying man may try to seize life by the throat, so the opposite often occurs when life returns to the sick. Desire, uncertain and afraid to seek an outlet, hesitates and then, as it awaits renewal, looks backward and instead of acting, remembers the past. As Mila recovered, she remembered.

They usually pastured the flock on some rugged slopes near Goblin Crest where a few rays of light would penetrate the clouds. The sheep scattered across the hills, always facing the sun, chewing the weeds that dotted the stony ground like tufts of green hair. Mussol also faced the light, his eyes half-shut, switching his tail against his haunches, while Baldiret blew the seeds off elder branches he had brought from the plain or rounded a stone ball he had been working on for months, hammering it repeatedly with an old broken horseshoe, and finally, Mila and Gaietà had long, leisurely conversations.

Forcing her to gaze over every steep precipice, teaching her how to twist her body and secure her footing in dangerous spots, making her look down when they were halfway up a cliff and laughing at her terror, he helped conquer her fears, held her when she was dizzy, and guided the woman through her mountain apprenticeship, winning out at last over her timorous, fawn-like nature. And now she loved the excitement she felt on those peaks and the way the yawning depths seemed to suck her soul out of her.

Sitting at the top of Nestwatch Mountain, thousands of feet above the plain, her cape thrown back and her legs dangling above the void, as clouds galloped overhead like herds of wild horses while the Black Ravine's huge, gaptoothed jaws opened below her, Mila felt perfectly at home, and perhaps because of these grandiose surroundings, tender memories returned from her youth.

Her gaze lost in the distant reaches of memory, she talked on and on while the shepherd, seated beside her whittling something for Baldiret or his sheep, listened attentively without interrupting: "If you could have seen my aunt...she was such a kindly soul! Her face was tiny, brown as a walnut, and her hair fell straight as a curtain from the part to each ear... She called the two sides her two armies. When I combed her hair I'd sometimes make a big curl on each temple, and then she'd pat my skirts behind, pretending to spank me. She loved me a lot, poor dear... No one would have guessed we were only related by marriage. When my mother died – may she rest in peace – she offered to take me in. My uncle had such bad kidney trouble that he could hardly work and didn't want the bother, but she told him: 'How can you turn away your own flesh and blood? What would you do if she was from my side of the family? I'm only her godmother but I love her like a daughter...' My uncle always teased her about the way she chose my name. He said she'd gone through I don't know how many calendars looking for a nice one, and finally chose Camilla because that's what the girl in the castle was called. 'And look,' he'd say as a joke, 'they'll both have it easy; one's got that castle and the other'll get my boat...,' because my uncle was a boatman, you know? Before they built the bridge, he used to ferry people across the river in a little white boat on a rope stretched from one bank to the other. Further up there was a ford where the wagons would cross, but the people always used his boat. It was nice to watch on Sundays and market days, when the boat was full of peasants in new caps that looked like red carnations. On St. Peter's Day, when all the fishermen celebrated, we'd decorate his boat with real carnations, roses, and any other flowers we could find. One year, when I was older and it was mostly me who looked after him, the boys from our village strung flowers around the boat and tied a big bouquet on top of his pole with blue and white elastic bands. They did it the night before and when we got there on St. Peter's Day, they were hiding in the bushes, waiting to hear what we'd say! It looked like a procession with all those flowers..."

Mila stopped for a moment, savoring the memory, and then sighed: "Rivers are such pretty things!"

"Everything's pretty if you look at it right, hermitess."

"Some things more than others...in my whole life I never saw anything as lovely as that river when the sun was setting. When no one was around I'd take the pole, push the boat halfway across, and stop there. The boat would rock like a cradle, so slowly it almost put me to sleep, and as I pushed it back I'd watch the sun like a burning flower behind those big poplars full of chirping birds, and I'd listen to the lumberjacks joking as they worked. Everything seemed far, far away...and I loved to watch the wagons splashing across the ford! I could have stayed there forever!...What can I say? ...I felt good, the way you feel in a big, empty church, and I'd start saying Paternosters for everyone in my family, dead or living... But the bridge ruined that river, and us too. In two or three years they'd chopped down all the best trees, people stopped using the ford, and they'd built a factory on the hill so that at dusk instead of all that peace and quiet, you know what we heard? The men who got off work at the factory made straight for the tavern, throwing rocks at the birds and singing dirty songs. And that poor little boat was sad to see, tied to the dock all by itself like a sick dog. My uncle refused to sell it and we sometimes took it out for fun — me, him, and my aunt — but you couldn't see anything with that bridge in the way, and my

uncle wept whenever he saw the people crossing, as if...
Believe me, it killed him. He already had kidney trouble,
and when he saw his boat lying there useless, he got
worse in a hurry. While he could still get around, he'd go
out in the morning and make for the river. Since we'd
stopped weeding the banks, the boat was overgrown with
bushes that covered it like an awning. He'd hide out
there, and a half-dozen people said they heard him
sobbing, but what's for sure is that he always came back
with red eyes and got mad if my aunt asked him what was
the matter. After a while he couldn't get farther than the
kitchen. Still, on St. Peter's Day he had them take him to
the river in a wagon and asked us to decorate the boat in
memory of other years. But we couldn't! It would have
been too sad to see that broken-down, mossy boat
covered with roses. That day he wasn't the only one who
cried... When he passed away, my aunt tried to sell it but
it was too late. It had been lying there so long and was so
shabby that it had sprung a dozen leaks. The wood was
rotten...The day they went to look at it, I met Matias. He
was with the manager, who'd wanted to buy it, and the
whole time his boss was bargaining, he never took his
eyes off me. It didn't take him long to propose. He
seemed like a good man, and my aunt didn't have long to
live. I'd have been all alone...so I said yes. God, if only I'd
known what I was getting myself into!"

Mila's reminiscences always stopped short when she
reached Matias, and seeing her fall silent and gaze
blankly into the ravine's somber depths, the shepherd,
who monitored her emotional ups and downs, saw that it
was time to spring into action. Laying aside the piece of
wood he was carving, he stretched and stood up: "Oof!
My whole leg was asleep! It's too cold to stay here. Why
don't we take a little turn?" and he smiled cheerfully at
the woman.

Mila raised her head to contemplate that dark-clad

figure outlined against the mountain, his feet on the ground and his head far above her, as though he had suddenly grown taller and now reached the sky. She laughed and also rose. The sheep were scattered far and wide, while Baldiret and the dog played busily together.

Gaietà quickly surveyed his flock and then made his way down one of the slopes, followed by the woman, who watched him point to places near and far.

"You see that last olive tree down there? A funny thing happened there a while back! There was a mighty lord in Llisquents who did nothing but enjoy himself. His favorite pastimes were ruining young girls, eating and drinking, and going hunting... One day he spied a girl named Marialena, who was sewing in front of her house. His men carried her off, he forced her to spend the night with him, and the next morning he threw her out of his castle. When she found herself thrown out like this, the girl turned around and shouted: 'Lord of Llisquents! You swooped down on me like a bird of prey, and may I hear you screech like one before I leave this world!' Then she disappeared, and no one knew what had become of her... Years later, another lord who had a castle in the Roquissos invited the one from Llisquents to go hunting on his estate. He arrived with all his servants, but in the course of the hunt, he lost sight of the others and finally came to that olive tree, where he spied the prettiest little deer you ever did see, standing right on top of that boulder over there. The Lord of Llisquents, who'd hunted in many places, thought to himself: 'This must be my lucky day! That looks like a roe deer that wandered down from the Pyrenees. I'll give it to my host as a present!' And since the deer didn't move, he loaded his crossbow and shot it, but the animal suddenly took a leap and started dashing up the mountain. The hunter thought: 'You won't get far with that arrow in your side,' and he followed it, but the deer ran like the wind and the next thing he knew he'd lost sight of his prey. He thought: 'It'll fall when it reaches the top. I'll rest awhile and then follow its trail.' But just then another roe deer appeared on the peak above him. 'What's that: doe or buck? It'll make an even better present!' He reloaded his crossbow and shot another arrow. It was a clear day, and he saw the arrow pierce the deer's neck, but instead of falling it took a leap just like the first one and fled up the mountain till it was out of sight.

"The hunter was amazed and ran after it as fast as his legs would carry him. He was huffing and puffing by the time he reached the top, but even though he looked everywhere, he couldn't find a trace of any deer, dead or alive. 'What the Devil's going on?' he exclaimed. 'I can't see any trees or rocks where they could hide. Where could they have gone? Unless they've leapt off the mountain above Wild Goat Falls!' But that was a good half hour away, and not even a roe deer could have run that far so fast. But the Lord of Llisquents was beginning to get impatient, and he wasn't the kind to think before he acted. All he cared about was giving his host those deer. So without worrying about how tired he got or how long it took, he groped his way from rock to rock to Wild Goat Falls, thinking: 'They must be lying there bleeding to death in the gorge, because they couldn't have gone far with those arrows in them.' By the time he reached the falls, he was more dead than alive. He looked all over but he couldn't find the deer. He was astonished. If that wasn't a miracle he didn't know what it was! He retraced his steps as carefully as if his life depended on it, but he still couldn't see a thing. He was about to give up and turn back, cursing Heaven and earth, when he looked up and saw another deer right at the top of Lookout Mountain, stretching its neck to sniff the breeze on either side. The lord shouted for joy and took careful aim. Then he noticed that this one was unwounded and much smaller than the others. 'It's their fawn! But what the Hell as long as I can bring it down!' Those deer had gotten under his skin so much that even if he lost the grownups, he'd be satisfied with the baby. But since it was so small and far away, he was afraid he'd miss and, rousing his forces, he clambered up the other side. Then he loaded his crossbow and shot it right in the belly. 'I've killed that one for sure!' cried the Lord of Llisquents, seeing it stumble, but then it righted itself and dashed away up Lookout Mountain. 'This is witchcraft!' thought the hunter, trembling from head to toe, 'but if I tell my host what happened he'll think I'm crazy or a liar. I've got to bring back those deer or never show my face again in his castle.' He looked at his clothes, which were in shreds from all the thistles, and at his shoes, which were so torn they left a trail of blood at every step, but he still had a spark of courage left, like the last embers in a dying fire. He started walking. Night began to fall, everything turned ashy gray, and finally he couldn't even see where he was going. He started stepping on burrs instead of stones. He kept stumbling as he climbed, and once he came to a cliff and had to retrace his steps. It was pitch black by the time he reached the top of Lookout Mountain. 'I must be crazy! I'll never spot those deer in the dark!' And without the strength to say another word, he fell in a faint.

"After a while, he was awakened by a distant echo. 'My friends must be searching for me,' he thought, and that idea gave him hope. He listened as hard as he could, but it seemed like the echo was churchbells instead of hunting horns. Then he looked all around and saw a faint glow in the west, all the way down at the foot of the mountain. As he looked, he felt his eyes swell and swell till they were as big and sharp as an owl's, and he saw a convent down below with a procession of nuns outside it. The bells tolled for someone who was dying, and the nuns walked two by two, holding candles and singing hymns as they went. A chill pierced the lord's heart and he tried to shut his eyes, but he couldn't because they covered his whole face and were big as saucers. In his fright he tried to cover his face, but he found that instead of arms he had two big wings covered with feathers that made a sound like the wind when he flapped them up and down... He tried to shout 'Help, Holy Virgin!' and all that came out was a long screech that echoed through the hills. He spread his wings and flew through the night till he reached a big gully above the convent. Nearby stood a huge fir tree almost two thousand years old. As he lit on one of its branches he saw a steeple below him, with its bells all tolling and a row of windows from the nuns' cells. One window was open, and through it he saw a white bed where a sister lay, holding a little statue of Christ in her hands. The nun was dying, the friar was hearing her last Confession, and the other nuns were singing hymns for her soul's salvation. As the hunter looked more closely, he saw that she was that girl he'd spent the night with years ago. Then he realized that God had punished him for his sins and started shouting from his fir tree: 'Forgive me, Marialena! Forgive me, I beseech you!' But he could hardly bear the sound of his own screeches, which woke every man and beast in these mountains. The nuns stopped singing, stared at the tree, and, dropping their candles, ran into the convent as fast as they could. The friar fell to his knees and crossed himself, and the dying nun turned in terror to look out the window, where she saw a huge bird dark as a shadow and twice as big as the biggest eagle you ever saw, with gigantic round eyes that shrank and swelled, bright as two blazing forges. The hunter saw she was looking at him and again tried to repent, saying: 'Oh, please take pity on my sinful soul, Marialena!' And he spread his wings like someone begging for mercy. Then the sick nun sat up and clasped her hands: 'Oh Almighty Savior, that must be the Lord of Llisquents who heartlessly threw me out of his castle! Now I can die happy, for he stole me from my nest and now I see him screeching like a bird of prey in the night...' And having uttered these words, she quickly passed away.

"The next morning, that lord opened his eyes and found himself lying on Lookout Mountain, with his clothes all in shreds and his feet caked with blood. Nearby he saw a shepherd looking down at him, while the mountains rang with the sound of churchbells. He stood up and started questioning the shepherd, who told him how the night before a wondrous miracle had occurred: 'A nun we worshipped as a saint died and went to Heaven, and all those bells are ringing in her honor... She was so saintly that the Devil, who'd never managed to tempt her, tried to trap her on her deathbed by appearing as a big owl, perching in a fir tree, and screeching as loud as he could to distract her from her last Confession. But it didn't work, and when he saw she'd go straight to her Maker, he got so mad there was thunder, lightning, and a smell of sulfur all through the mountains. That big old fir tree snapped like a twig, and the friar and those nuns are still shaking from the sight of Lucifer, may God preserve us from his wiles, Amen!'

"Then the lord asked the shepherd how he knew so much about it, and he replied that he'd heard it from another shepherd down below, who'd heard it from a woman who worked in the convent and had gotten the story straight from the sisters. She was going around telling people in all the nearby towns. The Lord of Llisquents did not wait to hear more and, repenting of his sins, he returned to his castle, where he gave each servant a hundredweight of gold. Then he donated all his wealth and lands to the convent at Cabrides, and, dressed in the clothes he'd worn on that hunt, followed the trails those three roe deer had led him down till he reached the gully, which people had started to call Owl Gully because of what had happened that night. Lightning had struck the fir, just as the shepherd said, and instead of roots there was a gaping hole in the ground. The lord made it his home, and even now people still call it Hunter's Cave in his memory... And the old folks say that sinner became such a wise and holy penitent that when the Pope had some difficult question to settle, he'd send a messenger to him and abide by his decision... Well, that's the end of the roe deer story, and the moral's behind the door, as Baldiret would say..."

By the time Gaietà had finished, Mila no longer recalled her marriage, nor did troubling memories disturb her peaceful recovery, and since the morrow would bring another tale, and still another the day after – for the shepherd's majestic flow of words seemed inexhaustible as the sea – Mila finally lost sight of her own stunted life as a simple human being and entered the mountains' fantastic realm. Spellbound by her friend's prodigious imagination, she watched the Roquissos' narrow confines grow till they encompassed entire worlds, full of visions, dreams, and fabulous monsters. From every field, rock, and branch a legend sprouted, and her sense of wonder blossomed into a new and higher awareness. At the same time, she felt an extraordinary devotion to that little man, whose ingenuity and kindness had lifted her to such heights.

One day when he had finished talking, she gazed at him adoringly and, putting all her admiration into a few words, asked: "Shepherd, where did you learn so many things?"

Gaietà smiled. "I never try to learn anything, hermitess."

"Then who taught you all those stories?"

The shepherd pushed back his cap, exposing his pale

brow crammed with glowing thoughts.

"The little ones I heard from the old folks at St. Pontius," he slowly replied, "and the rest...from Our Lord."

And seeing the woman continue to stare, he explained his puzzling answer: "When I find a new spot in the mountains, I sit down all by myself and take a good look at it, and while I'm looking, I can feel my heart begin to warm, and that warmth spreads till it reaches my head... And like some voice was telling me, I think of everything that must have happened there... And that's why I say it must be Our Lord, because who else could speak inside you when you're all by yourself?"

The creator's eyes shone with a firm conviction entirely free of vanity, while Mila felt that before this blessed soul, she was nothing but dust.

XIII. Highpeak

It was time for Gaietà to settle in at St. Pontius' Farm, where he and his sheep would spend the winter beneath the Nina's blue granite head. Knowing that without him Mila would be prey to all the worries that had once beset her, he postponed his departure time and again, but now he could wait no longer. The rains often prevented him from pasturing his flock, obliging him to spend idle hours in the kitchen, occupied in some trivial task or chatting with goatherds from Murons and Ridorta who had also taken refuge there. In addition, the people at St. Pontius had begun to complain, supposedly because Baldiret was absent from school but really because they needed his sheep manure for their crops, and even Anima, finding himself alone with Marieta on one of the Skeleton's slippery trails, told her not to expect Gaietà that winter, since with Matias out of the way, the shepherd had plenty of work to do at the hermitage. Marieta, deriving all the leverage she could from this slander, repeated it to Gaietà, who, though he merely chuckled at the time, nonetheless resolved to quit Mila's house. That night he told her. The two of them and Baldiret were eating supper by the hearth, and Matias either had not come in yet or – more likely – would not return that night.

Gaietà had just piled a few more kermes logs on the fire and, after bending over to see that they were firmly positioned, he turned to Mila: "Hermitess, you'll need a good supply of kindling when we're gone... Tomorrow me and the boy'll fight it out with those women from

Ridorta."

The woman spun around in her seat: "Are you going to leave so soon?"

The shepherd wedged the logs in tightly, slapping them with the palm of his hand. "Today's Saturday, isn't it? Well...around the middle of next week."

He wanted to say: "Monday or Tuesday," but his courage failed him. Mila flushed, mumbled "Oh really?" and felt her eyes fill with tears, while the man thought he saw her wipe them in the flickering darkness and turned away lest he find out for sure.

Baldiret was carefully cutting the panels from an illustrated broadside the rector had given him and paid no attention to the grownups' conversation.

The woman stammered: "But how can I live here all by myself?"

The shepherd stirred the fire, which rustled like crumpled paper. Since he didn't reply, the woman wondered if he had heard her. After a short pause, she continued in the same tone: "You promised to show me Highpeak..."

This time Gaietà responded: "And God willing, we'll do it! You wouldn't want to miss these mountains' crowning glory! From the Cross up there, you can see half the kingdom..."

"But if you're going to leave..."

"We've got a few days left...and it'll only take one. When would you like to go?"

"Well...with all the work I have to do..."

"Tomorrow's no good, 'cause we'll be in church. How about Monday?"

It rained all day Sunday, and Mila began to worry, but toward evening the sky cleared and Gaietà forecast good weather. They would rise in the dark, when the moon still shone like a white slash in the icy firmament.

Mila had spent a restless night, and her slightly

delirious state, in which she scarcely knew whether she was dreaming or thinking, had left her feeling tense and fearful. As she sliced half a round loaf of black bread upon her table, the shepherd warned her to dress warmly, because the early morning cold would cut like a knife.

Baldiret was hunched over near the fire, his hands in his pockets, yawning from ear to ear. That day, he was lord and master of the hermitage. Gaietà told him to gather the flock and lead it out if they weren't back in time.

The stars had nearly vanished by the time they set out, making their way across the fields that led to the first pine groves.

Behind them they heard Mussol barking for his master, while Baldiret's squeaky voice, calling "goodbye, goodbye" from the terrace, was mimicked by all the fairies' mocking echoes.

Gaietà had not been mistaken: the bitter cold seemed even sharper in the breaking dawn. It still had not snowed, but frost whitened the ground and made it look as though they were treading on splinters of broken glass. Five minutes after they lost sight of the hermitage, Mila's hands began to ache and, imitating Baldiret, she hunched over and buried her head between her shoulders. They approached the Roar, whose noisy waters, swirling in their basin and tumbling from rock to rock, carried the mountains' icy breath far and wide.

As they drew nearer, that noise, multiplied a hundred times by the dark hills, so frightened Mila that she clutched the shepherd's arm.

He walked along in silence, puzzling over God knows what. Feeling the woman beside him, he turned, but his smile was lost in the tenuous half-light.

"Ah!...it's great to be up and about so early, don't you think?" he gently asked, and without awaiting her reply, he stared fixedly in front of him.

Mila then recalled what she had so often felt before: that while she was near this man, whose presence she sensed so strongly, he was far away, oblivious, lost in his own thoughts.

This revelation always took Mila by surprise, making her pull away from him with a kind of awkward self-consciousness, and so it was on this occasion. After climbing a piney slope, they turned onto a goat path that wound around the craggy base of Roquís Gros. The woman let him walk before her in the shadows, while she followed close behind.

The first glimmers of daylight seemed to materialize imperceptibly in tiny particles, and their very pallor, more than the dark, filled the grove with ominous shapes, whose blurred outlines and proportions made everything as fantastic as Gaietà's stories. Mila turned her head from side to side, prey to an irrational fear that had tormented her as a girl. Sometimes she felt she was walking on air, and sometimes every cranny or patch of brambles concealed a skeletal hand that would tug at her skirts. And the pines, those bizarre silhouettes huddled together in clumps, seemed like evil apparitions that watched her pass and then wickedly stole after her. She wanted to flee into the woods, to escape...but she walked on till suddenly a heather thorn caught on her apron, startling her so that she couldn't help screaming and running to the shepherd, who nearly lost his balance, then halted in surprise and asked anxiously: "What's the matter, hermitess?"

"I don't know...nothing...I must be seeing things..." And ashamed of her fear, she blushed from head to toe.

Gaietà quickly regained his composure.

"Still scared of the dark, eh? I didn't know what to think, with that cry... So you haven't recovered yet? You're a sad case, I declare..."

And as though regretting his previous neglect, he

stayed by her side. The path was so narrow that their bodies sometimes brushed, and, thrilling with pleasure at that warm contact in the chilly air, she pulled her shawl even more tightly around her shoulders. They walked silently, white clouds of steam issued from their mouths and noses, and the crunch of their footsteps was the only sound audible.

The trees began to thin out and the path became still narrower, like the cleft between two breasts, as it made its way through the Roquissos, which rose like Cyclopean walls on either side, as though yearning to join and crush those human specks who dared to disturb their peace.

Feeling trapped and suffocated in that crevice, Mila turned her gaze toward the bushes spotted with white lichens, and then higher till she saw the sky's somber company. Near that patch of dark blue, she suddenly sensed, like a sonar phosphorescence, a restless chirruping that seemed suspended overhead, hovering above St. Pontius' Pass without the force to sink earthward.

"They call that the birdhouse," said Gaietà, looking up. "Don't go near the top of it now or at sundown. The birds'll peck your eyes out. There are thousands of them, y'see... They swoop down on the wheatfields and eat everything in sight..."

A little beyond the birdhouse, the wall on their right parted as though cut by scissors, and two toothlike rock formations stood out from the others, resembling huge prehistoric claws.

"What's that?" asked Mila as soon as she spied them.

"The Combs. Those two are the big ones, and there's a small one on the other side. You can see all three of them lined up from the top of Lookout Mountain, and since there's a gorge below, they call it Three Comb Gorge. In the old days, people say they were made of tarnished silver, and the fairies dipped them in a pond where they'd bathe kids they didn't like so their hair would turn white as snow before their time."

Gaietà, who was in no mood to talk, didn't expand upon this explanation, and they walked on in silence till a new sight piqued Mila's curiosity.

Till then the path had gradually descended, and right beneath the Combs, Mila and Gaietà reached its lowest point. The walls on either side spread outward like a "V," formed by overlapping rocks that resembled a monster's scaly skin. Water poured down them, as though it had just rained, and their shiny grayness reflected the pale sky's bluish light. The breaking dawn above their heads made the path seem even darker.

"It's so scary!" whispered Mila, gazing around and crossing her arms over her chest.

"We're in Lightningbolt Pass. If anyone's out to get you, keep away from this place, 'cause if they roll a rock down from the Combs it'll flatten you like a pancake. I stopped bringing the flock this way a while back... You have to watch out..."

The shepherd's brow furrowed as he uttered these solemn words. Mila, whose eyes had grown accustomed to the darkness, looked closely at the man's strangely gnarled features, which had assumed a hitherto unknown expression. She suddenly wondered: "What if he's talking about himself and will suddenly turn against me?" The idea made her feel faint, and she stopped in her tracks. Thinking it was the narrowness of the gully, Gaietà calmly walked ahead. His red cape, thrown over his shoulders, covered his neck and back, and the bulging pouch beneath the wool made him look like a hunchback. The woman's eyes, still large with fear, remained fixed on that back. No, the shepherd wasn't out to get her. She trusted him implicitly, but...and her suspicions took another, more circuitous route till once again she began to wonder, for...even the best men sometimes stumble and fall, swept away by passions that mock their best intentions. Everyone's a thief when he has the chance, the saying goes, and they were alone in that abyss. Only God knew they were there and could witness their deeds, but the wicked care little about hiding from God. They only worry about other people...

Mila shuddered and saw again in the darkness of that place the broad, warm, devoted, infinite gaze that had blotted out Arnau's red lips, breaking the current of attraction between them. That look had seemed a revelation, a promise... So why would it be strange if...? Her blood ran cold, and she realized that something dreadful might occur.

It was another moment of instinctive terror, but abruptly, as though a door had been flung open to reveal a grand ballroom, her eyes were dazzled by blinding light and tumult filled her ears. She looked into the depths of her soul and felt, without the shadow of a doubt, that if "it" were to happen, she would surrender without a fight. No: if that kindly man, high in the mountains or in the gorge's tempting darkness, were to approach and take her in his arms like a newborn baby lamb, she would not cry out, flee, or utter a word of resistance... No, no; she would meekly, joyously let herself be taken and cling to that sheltering bosom as she had so often longed to do. She would happily give that friend the light of her eyes, the fervor of her lips, her body's unused riches... Lost in that wondrous fantasy, she tasted his loving embrace and felt herself transported to those mysterious worlds he visited by himself.

The shepherd turned around: "God Almighty, are you ready to go home?"

Mila had fallen behind and finally stopped altogether. The man's words startled her like a pistol shot. She tried to smile and stared at Gaietà with the astonished gaze of one who contemplates something never seen before.

A dozen steps further on he awaited her, calm as

always and with a smile upon his lips.

The woman felt bitterly ridiculous in her own eyes. How could he want to hurt her? He would never be swept away by passion or try to bend her to his will! What nonsense!... The evidence of her delusion slapped her in the face like a shameful taunt. She knew she was beautiful, alluring, desired and desirable. First those vicious beasts at the festival, then the hunting parties from Barcelona, and her own restless longings had clearly proven it. So why did neither of those two men − Matias or Gaietà − to whom she would have given her love, not devour her like a sweet, ripe fruit? Matias considered her just another habit, devoid of charm or interest. No spark from the sacred fire had kindled that cold spirit, drawing the magic flame from its indifferent depths. And the shepherd? The shepherd neither felt nor wished to feel such a flame. Before, after the festival, he had treated her like Marieta, Baldiret, or even his sheep, acting as a sort of benevolent providence, sheltering everyone equally without distinctions.

Suddenly that providence touched the woman's arm, making her start with surprise.

"What're you so scared of? Anyone would think you were made of quicksilver! Try to be less jittery!..." and the man threatened her affectionately with his leathery hand.

"I was daydreaming," she confessed.

"I reckon you were! And when you're daydreaming you don't see or hear a thing. When I'm in some out-of-the-way place, I'd rather use my eyes than my tongue. You can't be sure who's watching, y'know? It'll be different once we're out in the open."

Mila then noticed two things she had missed before: first, the sun had risen, and second, they were about to emerge from St. Pontius' Pass. Twenty steps ahead, the wall on the right abruptly ended. Beyond it, she saw a patch of sky bright as a mirror, and atop the cliff, just before it vanished, a rugged crag arose, proud and airy as the tower on a medieval castle.

"That looks like the Moor's Boundary stone," said Mila, pointing to it.

"There's quite a difference, hermitess!" the shepherd replied. "The Boundary Stone's a grain of sand compared to that Jew on Windwhistle Heights... It must be ten times higher than the steeple at your hermitage, and if a man stood up there he'd look tinier than a mosquito. I scaled it years ago and almost lost my footing. It's as smooth as a pole and twice as hard to climb!"

Beyond the pass, the landscape rolled away into the distance, flowing toward far-off mountains tinged with the rainbow hues of Venetian crystal.

"How pretty the light is!" thought Mila, feeling her heart swell like the space before her and shaking off those demons engendered by the darkness. She raised her head and breathed in the cool splendor she beheld all around her. The morning air, which cut like a razor at those altitudes, attacked her head on, clinging to her face like a metal mask.

The shepherd stopped and leaned on his crook.

"See what a nice day it is? Not a speck of fog on earth or a wisp of cloud in Heaven. Lord love us, we couldn't have picked a finer morning! When we get to the top, we'll be able to see all creation..." And fascinated, he slowly gazed from side to side with the majestic serenity of a king born to the purple.

"You'll never guess what I feel when I'm up this high," said Mila, closing her eyes and throwing back her head.

"Mother of God! I'm sure I wouldn't know," replied the shepherd. "They say women are always full of strange notions."

"Yes, it is pretty strange... I can't see straight and the sky seems to spin like a water wheel, and when it's way down at the bottom like a reflection in a pond, I feel like diving in and drowning in the sky."

Gaietà looked at her curiously.

"I feel that way too, y'know. Except I want to fly like God's birds instead of sinking like a stone."

And they went on zigzagging up the mountain, seeking easy trails through the frosty scrub, kermes oak and rosemary, which looked as if they had been dusted with powdered sugar. Occasionally, Gaietà turned around to encourage his companion.

"Enjoying yourself, hermitess? Don't give up now; we're almost there."

"Listen, I'm no more tired than when we first started out, and the weather today's just perfect for walking!"

And in fact the woman, spirited as a soldier marching beneath his nation's banner, climbed vigorously, feeling a warmth in her breast that made the chilly air even more agreeable.

Galls like empty thimbles fell from kermes oaks as she passed, and rosemary branches brushed against her skirts, showering them with tiny crystals.

Mila then recalled her first ascent with Matias: so sad, so weary, so full of misgivings. How different from this one, which was so pleasant and refreshing, despite the winter cold, her poverty, and her blighted marriage! In a few months, everything had crumbled around her, yet only recently had she begun to feel strong and self-assured, clasping something that, willy-nilly, kept her afloat. "It's so important to have a friend!" she thought, gazing more calmly at the bent figure before her. The shepherd halted again.

"Look! There's King's Glass!" and he pointed down like a guide who knows the landscape by heart.

"God! It looks like a twisted paper cone!" exclaimed Mila in amazement. "Hey! Isn't that the Nina? And the farmhouse, and the Pont del Cop...?"

"That's right! And there's Pear Rock and Gallowseat and Olivebreath... All the places you pass on your way to Murons."

"They're so far from each other, but from here they look so close!"

And so they did. At the bottom of the cleft where the three Roquissos met, piled like the remains of a wine pressing in a funnel, was a miniature Nativity scene full of grottoes, trails, peaks, and modest man-made embellishments that seemed to await their admiring comments.

"See that tan ball that looks like it's rolling toward Olivebreath? That's Pear Rock. If you put your ear to the ground when it's just been raining, you'll hear a roar underneath like a raging lion..."

"And what is it, shepherd?"

"Who knows, hermitess! Folks say these hills are full of caves and tunnels, like a giant anthill, and that noise is the sea, which echoes through the mountains."

Once Mila had drunk her fill of the scene, they made their way up the slope on their right, sometimes advancing and sometimes seeming to retreat, but always climbing, climbing, and as they climbed ever higher, the mountains opened before them, revealing all those places in the shepherd's tales. Perhaps they were not as fair and grandiose as in his stories, but the day was so sunny, the hour so enlivening, the ascent so enjoyable that Mila found everything delightful.

Once, as they were making their way eastward, a sort of green velvet cape appeared below them, with its hem crumpled against the mountain's base, a grayish half-circle like a thrown-back hood, and, around that hood, a short, reddish border.

"Does that look familiar?" asked Gaietà, pointing to the cape. The woman scrutinized it for a while.

"Why, that's the hermitage!" she shouted with childish

glee. "It looks so tiny! There's the terrace and the roof on the kitchen...and the belfry, long and white like a goose's neck...and the yard and the pine groves... Which are those thick ones: the first or the second?"

"The first ones! Can't you see the Dragon's Head, sticking its nose through the trees by the Roar?"

"Of course, of course! I can even hear the water..." She turned to the shepherd and asked: "Why didn't you bring me here before? It's the prettiest spot in these mountains..."

"Well, you see all those black kermes oaks? The goatherds from Murons singe them so there'll be more buds in the spring, but that means the animals can't eat the leaves in the winter. That's why I always go up the other side. It's more peaceful over there, and I don't get into so many fights..."

Mila stared at him.

"What do you think the boy's doing now?"

"Milking the sheep so he can have breakfast," Gaietà replied, and then added, "or toasting some bread on the fire. There's a wisp of smoke rising from the chimney..."

And both of them, he and she, enveloped in a wave of tenderness, imagined that child whom for the first time they had abandoned, perhaps impelled by an unspoken wish to be alone together.

In fact, during those long, erratic wanderings that had marked Mila's recovery, so full of secret pleasures and yearnings, Baldiret had more than once been a source of irritation, with his ill-timed eruptions, deafening shouts, and boyish pranks. Though undiminished, her love for him had grown less urgent, as if womanly feelings had supplanted her maternal instincts. Unconsciously, she had often longed for one of those idylls far from everything and everyone that lovers dream of, and doubly so since instinct, if not calculation, seemed to suggest that only thus could she breach Gaietà's reserve, forcing something important and irrevocable to occur. But events rarely conform to our expectations, as she now had to concede. She and her beloved had been alone, in sweet isolation, yet despite all her hopes and fears, nothing had happened. Except for one brief moment in Lightningbolt Pass, when she had surrendered to dark imaginings of which she now felt ashamed, their hike had been exactly the same as all the others, or perhaps calmer, more innocent, freer of unuttered passions. Yes, that was all that had really occurred. But even so, her heart felt lighter than ever before.

The shepherd seemed to answer her thoughts. Tired of watching her stare down at that bird's-eye view of her home, he clapped his hands to break her trance, exclaiming: "How about moving on, hermitess? You looked so dreamy I hated to disturb you, but the sun sets early this time of year and if we stay too long, we'll never get back in time."

"Yes, you're right. Lets go...and whenever I stop give me a good pinch. This mountain's put a spell on me!"

"Didn't I say it would, back when you were moping around? You have to take things as they come and not fly off the handle..."

"Can I help it if I'm not as slow as you?" she retorted, amused at her own sharp tongue.

The shepherd laughingly replied: "That's the way I like to see you, not with your head tucked under your wing like before! Thank God you've finally come to your senses!"

"That's your doing," she answered, serious once more.

"Come on, don't make me laugh! It was glorious St. Pontius!"

"Forget about St. Pontius; he couldn't care less. You did it with your stories, which show the good side of everything... If it wasn't for you, I'd have died in these hills and been buried beside that old hermitess under a flagstone in the courtyard."

Gaietà didn't reply because a few yards away he saw a young man with lowered head who was climbing the rocky slope, holding a switch in his right hand while the left swung back and forth like a pendulum. Behind him a herd of goats with mischievous faces and twitching beards kicked up their heels and straggled among the rocks.

As they passed, the shepherd said: "Hello there."

"Morning, Gaietà."

"You're out early today."

"I can't help it! They kick up such a fuss inside!"

"Well, that's how they are... Take it easy."

"So long, Gaietà."

And he receded into the distance, humming to himself.

"I'd love to be a goatherd!" Mila exclaimed.

"Like him?" the man scornfully replied. "Those loafers think it's a way to get by without working. I'd like to get my hands on them... I hate to see them lying around in the shade in summer and the sun in winter, napping in some field as if they were sick, without a care in the world or a thought in their empty heads. They either starve their flocks to death or let them eat till they burst, and not only that but they throw stones at them too... They're good for nothing, you understand? It's a shame to let young people carry on like that, 'cause the way they are now is how they'll be all their lives!"

And the shepherd's usually benign visage grew solemn and severe.

Then they spied King's Glass again in the west, though from a far greater height and looking slightly altered, but still like a deep cleft with a Nativity scene at the bottom, and the Three Combs, jutting up into the clear blue sky, and then Lightningbolt Pass, like a huge gash beneath Windwhistle Heights, and far away, a jumble of muddy colors that were the fields on the plain.

Mila stopped a moment to ask: "Tell me shepherd: is

there any other way to reach the top?"

"Sure there is! These mountains are full of trails and you can take any one you like..."

"Without going through Lightningbolt Pass?"

"Only if you don't mind climbing straight up, but that's not for ladies, or you can try the pass at Ravens' Nest...over there in the east, on the other side of the Roquissos..."

"Really? Then let's go down that way."

"Well, okay, if you want to, but it's a pretty straight drop and you won't get much of a view."

"I don't mind. I'm sure I'll like it anyhow."

The shepherd laughed: "I can see what you're up to! You want to know these mountains inside out."

"That's it, shepherd."

"All right; then let's do it... You're strong enough, and you might even enjoy slipping down the Skeleton."

Mila wanted to avoid Lightningbolt Pass, the only blot on that wonderful day. She didn't mind gripping the rock with her fingernails, if by so doing she could avoid those troubling thoughts that had darkened their ascent.

And they went on climbing, turning left and right. The woman's eyes, eager for horizons, beheld the broad ridge of Roquís Mitjà and looked beyond it, lighting briefly on the distant plain. The Husk, like a meteorite fallen from Heaven, grew smaller and smaller till it seemed a tiny mound, as did Roquís Petit with its smooth plateau around the Boundary Stone. The golden sun beat down brilliantly upon the columned cliff before them, which the shepherd called the Organ because of its thick pipes. Finally, when at last they could look out on all sides, Gaietà stopped, peered at something, and motioned her to be still.

Mila obeyed, watching with surprise as he searched for a round stone, and, after choosing one, assumed a graceful pose and brought his right arm through the air.

The stone whizzed away, and where it landed something brown leapt up and then fell to earth. All this happened in a flash, and when Mila realized what Gaietà had done, he was holding a furry animal by the neck.

"God's with us today! Look at this fat hare I caught napping. He's about to molt and'll be tender as they come."

Held by its ears, its head split and covered with blood, the animal, still shaken by spasms, jerked its hind legs wildly. The wind blew back its fur, exposing lines of skin beneath the pelt, which was an inch long and fine as thistledown. Gaietà thumped the beast a few times on the ground to ensure that it was dead and told the woman, who was still staring, about the customs and character of hares.

"Strange beasts! Quick as lightning and even jumpier than you are. They're scared of their own shadows, and if anything startles them they're off like a shot. But sometimes they get tired of running away all the time, and then one of them'll leap right into your path. When a hare's worn out, it'll find a spot with a good view, curl up by a rock or bush that'll keep off the wind, and sit there so still you'd think it was dead. They can't see or hear a thing... Lots of times I've gotten close enough to touch them and they haven't budged an inch. I don't like killing animals, but since if I don't someone else will, I forget about that and aim a rock at their heads..." And he laughed, but upon seeing the woman's troubled expression, he added: "Come on now, don't be a crybaby! After all, it's no worse than your mother-in-law's funeral, and when you sink your teeth into one of those thighs, you'll agree it was better dead. There's quite a difference between a slice of toast and roast hare for breakfast... and I reckon this one'll be sweeter than a sixteen-year-old girl."

Mila quickly recovered, and they decided to cook the

hare when they reached the cliff. As the animal grew stiff and cold, they walked and talked together. At every few steps, Mila laughed without knowing why, and her gaiety rang through the hills and valleys like the sound of rushing water.

They soon reached the Organ, whose striated rock had been scored by many rainfalls. Facing east, the cliff offered shelter to the couple, who had been walking in the shade, touched by only a few rays of the sunlight that now beat down upon them with magnanimous abundance. As soon as Mila felt that caress upon her cold-reddened hands, she recalled a similar impression on her first trip up the mountain: her arrival at the Boundary Stone after the trek up Legbreak Creek. But it had been spring then, and however pleasant the warmth, it was far more delightful now amid the icy blasts of winter. As soon as Mila stopped, she happily shut her eyes, stretched her neck, and with a joyful moan, offered first one cheek and then the other to the sun, which kissed the smooth skin above her well-wrapped body.

"Looks like you're having a good time!" said her companion, beholding her ecstasy.

"Ooh, that feels wonderful!" she replied. "When we were walking, I thought nothing could be nicer, but I didn't realize how cold I was getting. My feet are frozen..."

"Well, no wonder... The ground's wet, and with those flimsy shoes you women wear, it's hard to believe they're really made of leather! Y'know what you should do? While I build a fire, take off your shoes, leave them in the sun, and rub your feet till they start to warm up."

Mila quickly followed his advice. She removed her shoes, rubbed her white feet with her socks till the skin turned pink, and sat barefoot on the warm ground, soaking up the sun's rays, while she enjoyed the tingling sensation in her veins. Resting on that plateau, she

watched Gaietà gather firewood and held the hare's legs
as he knelt to skin it.

Never in her life had Mila felt so happy. Her lips, eyes,
soul, and the mountains around her all smiled in unison.
Till, amid that surge of joy, she suddenly longed to kiss
someone... Involuntarily, tremulously, she turned to the
shepherd, whose bare head, bent over the hare, offered
its brow to her lips, but before she could complete the
action, something made her stop short. Without knowing
why, without having heard the slightest noise, she and
Gaietà both looked up in alarm. They gasped. There,
above the Organ's pipes, another head peered down at
theirs, hastily recoiled, and vanished without a trace. It all
happened in a flash, as if they had imagined it, yet the
pair remained frozen and unblinking for more than a
minute, still seeing that dark head with its white
jackal-fangs, as though the image had been stamped upon
the sky.

Gaietà was the first to rouse himself. His face
hardened with the cruel resolve of one who fights to the
death, he gripped his cap and gnashed his teeth to cool
his first murderous rage. Then he looked into the
woman's eyes.

"Did you see that?" he slowly asked. "All morning
long I've been expecting him. I was sure he was following
us. But...," and his face suddenly flushed, "he'd better
keep away or I swear to God I'll kill him!"

And with one deft slash, he ripped open the
hare's belly.

XIV. On the Cross

All their happiness had fled with that apparition.

After skinning the hare, Gaietà made a circle of stones, over which he laid a grill of woven branches from a nearby tree, and on that grill he placed the hare, spread open like a book and rubbed with garlic and a little olive oil. The animal cooked in its own juices, while the picnickers sat staring at the ground, lost in their own thoughts. They devoured it hungrily but joylessly, and that breakfast, which the shepherd had proclaimed sweeter than a sixteen-year-old girl and which would have indeed been so without the shock that had preceded it, was merely the satisfaction of a physical need.

From time to time, Mila raised her head to see whether the spy had returned, till at last Gaietà said: "Now for God's sake, stop worrying! He won't bother us again today, and even if they searched this whole mountain they wouldn't find hide nor hair of him... He sneaks around after people as long as no one spots him, but as soon as they do it's like the earth swallowed him up... Look how he's stayed away ever since he stole those rabbits... But someone's got to put a stop to it, and if he doesn't come to me, I reckon I'll have to go out looking for him..."

Holding a piece of meat she was about to bite into, Mila exclaimed: "Shepherd, for the love of God, leave that man alone! Don't say anything to him..."

"Go on, eat, and put it out of your mind. This is my business... "

"What makes him so nasty? He never frightened me before, but now I'm starting to feel scared."

"You've got nothing to worry about as long as I'm alive. He's always been as terrified of me as Satan is of crosses, and he's never even dared to look me in the eye... He doesn't mind taking your rabbits, since Matias is his friend, but he'll keep away from you 'cause he knows I'd never forgive him!"

Gaietà spoke in anger, but his words went straight to Mila's heart. Feeling her throat tighten, she could only reply: "Oh shepherd..., " while two big tears rolled down her cheeks.

The shepherd blinked in bewilderment, like a sleeper awakened by the morning light: "What's the matter, hermitess? Don't fuss so much or you'll make me mad!" And forcing a laugh, he added: "You pay too much attention to what I say and don't take things like I mean them... Sometimes a man can forget he's talking to a woman... But look, why don't we think about something else? Put away those napkins and let's get going, or they'll come looking for us with lanterns!" And after scattering the bones and stamping out the fire, he crammed everything into his pouch and was ready to go.

"He loves me, he loves me!" the woman thought to herself. "He's too shy to say so and doesn't want me to know, but he loves me!"

With tears in her eyes, Mila imagined what life would have been like if she had only met this man before the other one. But the die was cast, and what might have been happiness was now nothing but a sin. Yes: ever since they had seen Anima's head, this cruel thought had tormented her. What had they been doing wrong beneath God's vast blue sky? Nothing, of course! Yet all the same, she was so unnerved by Anima's evil leer that she would have given half her life to escape it. His eyes had sought to violate what he thought was a stolen moment.

They had nothing to hide, but he believed they did, and Mila felt crushed by his suspicions, as though she had been caught in a real sin. Perhaps what most distressed her was the fact that she had half-committed one, in thought if not in deed, for a sinner is he who bears the seeds of sin within him. Yet even so, by what quirk of fate should something now be wrong that in another time and place would have been pure and noble? And, her mind hopelessly adrift in a sea of confusion, the woman strained to grasp the hidden laws behind that phenomenon. She could not discover them, nor could she free herself from fear and uneasiness. One thing, however, was clear: the joy of loving freely was denied her, and pleasure seized on the sly was filth and wickedness... It was almost better neither to have nor to desire such pleasure! Better to love as they loved, fruitlessly and distantly. Though their love was unfulfilled, it was at least clean and honest...

And now Mila, again buffeted by turbulent emotions, admired what she had cursed in Lightningbolt Pass: the reserve with which Gaietà chastely veiled his inner feelings. Because he loved her, he loved her! She neither would nor could doubt it. His eyes had not deceived her that morning after St. Pontius' festival. He cherished her above all else and sought to shield her from harm!... And intoxicated by this thought, she repeated it to herself, fixing it in her mind as a drowning sailor might clutch a plank.

After walking awhile, they reached another ledge near the top of Roquís Gros, though they were still on the north side of the mountain. They made their way around some cliffs, and gazing upward, beheld the huge High-peak Castles above an abyss of waterfalls and escarpments: a ferocious cornice of stone worn smooth by the centuries, like a ruined barbican atop the Roquís' ancient fortress. Mila instinctively ducked as they passed beneath, as though fearing to see those cliffs come crashing down from their precarious perch. But the Castles remained as they had been for centuries, firm and motionless, seeming to laugh at her fear of those narrow paths that cut across the sheer rock beneath their ornate towers. The one in danger was Mila who, turning a sharp corner, saw the ground fall away, leaving nothing but sky.

She leapt back, while the shepherd smiled at her fear.

Mila felt that one more step would send her hurtling down that steep slope, at whose edges weeds and rosemary bushes bristled darkly against the light. Where was the rest of the mountain? Where had the world gone? They had been sucked into the brilliant void, which seemed to tug at her too as she stood at its brink with Gaietà beside her.

"Shepherd!... Shepherd!... " she cried, holding out her arms and feeling her head spin.

But almost before she could open her mouth, Gaietà had gripped her arm.

"Watch out! This is no place to fool around! From here to the top, the path'll be open on one side, and any nonsense will send you tumbling straight down that cliff. "

Mila quickly adjusted to the change, and following the shepherd's advice, kept her eyes on the ground. She felt the void, sometimes behind her and sometimes at her side, while her eyes glimpsed vertiginous ravines full of mirages, but she forced herself not to look down and picked her way among the burnt kermes oaks, whose charred branches brushed her skirts and clawed at her legs.

They didn't stop till the shepherd sighed and then exclaimed: "God Almighty! Here we are!"

They were at the Cross. A great rocky plateau crowned the mountain, flattening it like the top of a bushel of grain. At first Mila, who stood facing the center of that plateau, saw nothing more than stony ground dotted with the usual stunted bushes. A gust of wind pushed her forward and disheveled her hair.

"Mother of God!" she exclaimed anxiously.

"There's nothing to break the wind here; that's why it sweeps across so fast. But now that it's passed, take a deep breath. Everything smells like incense, pretty girls, and the sea..."

Indeed, the mountaintop smelled sweet as a rose. From time to time, invisible clouds enveloped them, drenching their senses in delightful aromas. Where did they come from? From the mountains and valleys, from the world below, which sent forth its purest breath while reabsorbing its more poisonous smells. But where was that world?

Gaietà seized her shoulders and spun her around.

Mila clapped her hands over her eyes and felt the roots of her hair tingle. Her memories of the Boundary Stone, Nestwatch, and all the mountains' other peaks: how small and pathetic they seemed to her now! This was vastness, this was boundless immensity!

She scarcely needed to ask if that tiled patch of ochre and sienna was Murons, the ancient town crisscrossed by dark streets. The smoke from its chimneys, mingling with the air, hung like a bluish cloud above the rooftops. Those rectangles in every shade of green were its fields and orchards. That silver strip beyond them was the river, a diminutive Nile that gave the town its fertility and whose banks were lined with naked poplars, beyond which she saw a stretch of brown wheat fields. Still further away, around Roquesalbes, she spied some gray and amber hills that were sprinkled with white hamlets like tiny grains of aniseed. The range veered right and ended in a high cliff, while on the left it was joined by darker and loftier mountains, which in the distance seemed to fill the entire south. That dark barricade's summit was flecked with patches of pinkish white so brilliant that they seemed to pierce the woman's eyes.

"That snow never melts," Gaietà replied to her question. "No matter what time of year you're here, you can see those snowcapped mountains. They're worth the climb all by themselves."

But Mila was less enthusiastic than the shepherd. She preferred the miniature scenes she could recognize below her.

From that plateau atop Roquís Gros, the highest peak in the area, she quickly spotted Roquís Petit, like a cap lying at its big brother's feet. A band of fields encircled Ridorta, perched upon its pretty hill, while a patchwork quilt of orchards, roads, and valleys led to Llisquents' terraced slopes, distinguished from afar by the glittering bell in its steeple. She saw Torrelles' cylindrical columns, blotches of sandy lowland, and much, much more in that limitless panorama...

They walked till they could gaze upon the steep ravines below them and on Roquís Mitjà's long, furrowed crest, like an intestine protruding from a huge stone stomach. Beyond it a dusty plain led to more pale blue mountains, and a few steps further, they were looking out toward the east.

Dazzled by a sudden flash as from a mirror, Mila shut her eyes. What was that long strip of blinding light on the horizon? Gaietà replied with a single word:

"The sea!"

Mila turned away as though someone had struck her.

Could that really be the fathomless sea she had heard of so often?

She blinked and rubbed her eyes; then she looked again, forcing herself to endure that brilliant glitter.

The sea! The sea she had always longed to behold! The sea of fish, shipwrecks, mermaids, conches and rainbow grottoes!... She remembered the votive offerings in the chapel, Gaietà's stories, those sayings and tales she had listened to as a child, everything about that celebrated mystery... A sense of disappointment crept over her.

Gaietà saw the disillusionment in her face and tried to kindle her enthusiasm. Mila politely pretended to be convinced, though she could not grasp the connection between all those words and a slender stream that looked like a giant's sword in one of the shepherd's fairy tales, nor did it resemble the mighty sea of her dreams, full of portentous legends. Losing interest, she began to stroll about once more, examining the ruins of the convent at Cabrides, the Moorish kings' ancient castle, which seemed to crumble down its rocky slope toward Murons, the jagged, pitted slopes on the side near the plain, and the wreath of olive trees around Roquís Mitjà's veiny base... Suddenly she remembered something and asked the shepherd: "But where's the cross? I haven't seen it."

He replied: "The Cross? Once upon a time, it stood on that peak."

"And now?"

The man looked at her in surprise.

"Now it's nowhere. But you must have heard about the Cross!" And seeing Mila shake her head, he briefly told the story.

"Five or six hundred years ago, there was a terrible plague in Murons. Jesus Christ bore away half the souls living there. People died like flies in the streets and squares, but no matter how many they buried there were always more corpses. They did everything they could think of to drive away the plague. Incense, processions,...it was all a waste of time. But since nothing lasts forever, one day the plague ended. Then the survivors decided to thank God for sparing them and gave what they could to make an iron cross so big you could see it from every village in these parts. Once it was ready, they swore to bring it up here themselves, and to please God even more, to follow the paths along these cliffs. And that's just what they did. Yellow and sickly, some from the plague and others from grief, rich and poor, great and humble, they all got together and, taking turns, they carried that cross right to the top. They stopped when the sun went down and spent the night eating, praying, and watching over it. It took them five days to climb the mountain, on the sixth they planted their cross, and on the seventh, which happened to be Sunday, they held a big celebration. There was a fellow in Murons who didn't believe in God and was so wicked that no one wanted to be his friend. He went to the celebration and, standing in the middle of the crowd, said something was missing: Jesus Christ, but he'd fix that in a jiffy. And before anyone could stop him he'd climbed the cross, while the people all yelled and shoved below him, and hung a mule's skeleton on it for everyone to see."

"Sweet Jesus, Mary, and Joseph," Mila sighed.

"But his punishment was swift, hermitess! As soon as he'd defiled the cross, while the bones were still rattling, though the sky was as clear and calm as today, a huge lightning bolt came down with such a mighty clap of thunder that everyone fell to the ground and covered their eyes. And when they slowly raised their heads, they saw no trace of that heathen or the cross. All that remained was the mountain and a mighty stench of sulfur. And that's how the Highpeak Cross was put up and knocked down. Nowadays, when people find some old whitened bone and can't tell where it came from, they bury it deep underground, saying: 'Go, heathen bone, and make Hell your home.' But if they find pieces of iron, they think they're from the Cross and hang them above their beds to ward off evil thoughts. I don't have a bed, y'know, so I keep a piece in my pouch..." Then Gaietà dug around in his bag, pulled out a rusty lump of metal, and showed it to the woman.

She asked skeptically: "You mean to say that's from

the Cross?"

"Everyone around here says it must be. I found it on the ground one day and I've kept it ever since. Who knows? At least it won't do me any harm..."

Mila wondered if Gaietà's serenity might not derive from that amulet rather than his own nature.

"What no one can doubt is the noise from the skeleton. Now and then it makes a sound just like when he hung it up there, whenever something bad's about to happen in these hills. I've heard it twice: once when my wife was about to die, and once when a piece of the Nina slid onto the stable at St. Pontius and buried the cows alive."

Mila smiled, and her twinkling eyes betrayed her incredulity. Sometimes Gaietà behaved like an overgrown child who believed all his own tales.

They walked on till at last, tiring even of splendid views and sweet aromas, the man asked if she would like to sit awhile before starting downward.

"It's about nine o'clock now. We can rest a little, go through the pass, and be home by ten."

Mila's eyes widened. "Only nine? How can that be? We've been walking so long..."

The shepherd calmly seated himself, with an arm around one knee and his other leg stretched out before him on the ground.

"Well...what time do you make it?"

The woman vainly tried to calculate.

"Don't worry, I'll figure it out for you. Coming straight up here takes a little less than two hours. All the rest was looking and stopping for breakfast."

Mila couldn't believe her ears. Altogether, they had been gone some four hours, though she would have guessed at least six or seven.

She sat down near the shepherd, still troubled, as he was, by Anima's appearance. They gazed down absentmindedly at Murons, surrounded by its patterned fields. Breakfast had been consumed and the wisps of smoke had vanished; only occasional long columns the color of whisky and water remained, like impalpable stibnite pillars on a fabulous temple bereft of its portico, dome, and pediments. Beneath the sun, which still cast long shadows, they saw tiled rooftops like scalloped shells in the distance, while figures no bigger than fly-specks made their way across the squares.

Mila's sharp eyes sought the places she knew best: France Street, where she sometimes went shopping, the open market, the big church, the rectory, the promenade, the fairground where livestock was sold and bartered... The church stood out because of its size and because it faced the sun. With its squat twin belltowers, its two round windows, and its red door among the shadows, it bore a certain resemblance to a colossal barn owl. As they looked, nine slow peals wafted upward from the town.

Mila suddenly wondered if Matias could be down there, and she quickly repeated her thought to Gaietà.

The shepherd shook his head. "I doubt it...he's probably still asleep."

Mila was surprised: "Asleep at this time of day? You must be joking."

The shepherd looked at her and seemed to hesitate.

"Well, you see...," he finally mumbled. "I didn't want to tell you because I thought you'd take it badly, but...maybe you should know...since I won't be around."

"What is it, shepherd?" exclaimed the woman, alarmed by that preamble.

"I told you I'd keep an eye on your husband, didn't I? Well, I kept my word and..."

"And?" she anxiously repeated.

"And he's not begging for the saint."

"Is that all? I already figured he wasn't. He tags along

after Anima...," she replied with a forced smile.

"He tags along after him...but not to hunt rabbits. Listen: when I go to Mass on Sunday I can find out anything I want to know just by asking the right questions, however well it's hidden. Your husband, nowadays, is a gambler by trade. All night he rolls the bones till the sun begins to shine, and then he sleeps all day in that bastard's den."

Mila was astonished.

"Matias, a gambler?"

If anyone else had said so, she would have called him a liar, but this was the shepherd and he wasn't one to gossip. She knew how carefully he weighed his words.

She stared at Gaietà, waiting to hear more.

"You remember how he used to be before? A brood hen, a loafer you couldn't smoke out of his nest... If you hadn't been there, the moths would have eaten him. I swear, every time I saw him I used to start worrying... But one day he slung that chapel over his shoulder, went out begging, and a week later he'd changed more than if they'd baked him again from scratch."

"That's true!" Mila exclaimed.

"I was afraid that change wouldn't be for the better, and when I saw him working for Anima I reckoned he was a goner. Anima knows how to sing all kinds of songs for his supper, and not only that but he can smell money a mile away. Your husband was like an empty house, and he moved right in. They drank up what they made selling rabbits and slept it off at his place... Matias was an easy catch. Anima's a born crook, and lucky too... Matias won a few rolls, and from then on they've been partners."

Staring down, Mila listened and also followed her own thoughts: Matias' deeds, words, fears and confusions, bits of his life that had seemed strange or trivial and that only now fell into place...

"A gambler! But he was such a lazy good-for-nothing!

Who would have thought...?"

The shepherd also gazed down, as though bewitched by the town below them. "You being too sick to care didn't help either one of you. You might have bullied him into holding off for a spell...but I'm not even sure of that, because when you're as big a fool as he is... Anyhow, you gave him all the rope he needed..."

The woman clasped her hands and stared at him despairingly.

"What could I do? I was more dead than alive!"

"Now, now, hermitess. I'm not trying to blame you. I just said what I thought..." And those calm eyes offered her unconditional absolution.

They fell silent again. Matias, Anima, that hermitage... laziness, quarrels, penny-pinching, loneliness...painful memories swarmed buzzing through heads that a moment ago had been cooled by Highpeak's pleasant breezes..., till the shepherd, whose gaze was still fixed upon Murons, said uncertainly: "Those damn towns are the cause of it all! Dens of iniquity... I'd rather have one rock in the mountains than a hundred houses down below...and without them you'd have less souls in Hell and less families in trouble... Those narrow streets make me feel like a lost sheep searching for a patch of sky. When I was still young, long after my wife died, they asked me to run a butchershop. It was a good living, but I wouldn't hear of it though it was nothing like now: thirty-five years ago there weren't so many houses of ill repute..."

Surprised, Mila asked: "Did you say thirty-five years ago? How old are you, shepherd?"

The man turned to her and smiled: "What's your guess, hermitess?"

"Me? Well, I would have thought...around forty..."

Despite his mood, Gaietà roared with laughter.

"God Almighty, that's not much, is it? Ha, ha, ha!... But you're joking, right?" And seeing her puzzled expression, he laughed even harder. "May St. Lucy improve your eyesight, and meanwhile, if we see someone selling spectacles, I'll buy you a pair with nice, thick lenses."

"What do you mean, shepherd?"

"Either you missed by a mile or you forgot how to count..."

"Well then..."

"God willing, I'll be sixty-four next January."

That day Mila had endured every kind of strong emotion, but none, neither her fear in Lightningbolt Pass and beneath the Organ nor what she had learned about Matias' doings, had struck her with such force. Nor could she feign indifference. The color drained from her cheeks and she stubbornly refused to believe the shepherd's words. Mistaking her protests for simple amazement, he counted the years on his fingertips, citing dates and recollections.

The woman heard nothing, while troubling thoughts winged through her head, beating more violently than the fiercest summer dust storm.

What strength! What peace of mind! What a sturdy old man! She clutched and unclutched her hands, feeling the blood pound in her knuckles. Sixty-four! What a grotesque mistake... And as long as they were on Highpeak, she remained trapped in this vicious circle.

After reminiscing a while longer, the man returned to Matias, about whom he tried to caution and advise her.

"Don't lose hope..., you never know..., try pampering instead of scolding... Beg him not to leave you alone. Maybe he'll decide..."

Mila heard these exhortations without understanding them, and the stiff wind that whipped her apron quickly scattered them far and wide. Finally, Gaietà noticed her distraction and, seeing her shudder from head to toe, asked: "Are you feeling sick, hermitess?"

"Yes... no... I'm a little chilly..."

He immediately rose to his feet.

"My God, why didn't you say so? I'm not a mind reader, y'know? Come on, let's get going."

The sea flashed in the distance like a band of gleaming steel. Mila glanced at it and looked away, thinking bitterly: "You can't believe anything... It's all lies and fairy tales."

They started down the east slope. There was not a flat inch in that network of ridges and gullies. People called it the Skeleton because its protruding layers of rock resembled the bones on some monstrous ribcage. The peasants went there to pick medicinal herbs, with which they made teas and poultices for themselves and their livestock. On that slope Anima had met Marieta as she returned with some herbs and had sought to poison her mind about Gaietà and Mila. As the shepherd remembered, his desire for revenge flared up like a bonfire fanned by a sudden gust of wind.

Mila followed close behind the shepherd, whom her eyes never left. Shocked by her recent discovery, she had quickly regained her eyesight and no longer needed glasses of any shape or kind. The ridged slope allowed her to scrutinize his head three or four feet below her, and although his beardless face and short chestnut hair were deceptive at first glance, if one looked more closely his age was perfectly obvious. That same hair had grown dull and faded with the years. His skin clung to the bones, and between them was as wrinkled as old parchment – in the hollows of his cheeks, for example, or the folds behind his ears. His nails were hard as a raven's claws, and his joints were slightly stiff. No, there was no doubt: he was not what he had seemed.

She compared him to her husband, who was young but old in spirit, while the other was an old man who looked much younger than his years. Both were freaks, and freakishness was the bane of her existence, blighting and destroying the very life within her breast... She again felt the black despair of one unfairly punished. Everything was hopeless! And she bit her lips till they bled, while her head spun dizzily.

Why not miss her footing and end it all, hurtling down that rocky slope? But even as the thought crossed her mind, she carefully took one step and then another...

In certain especially dangerous spots, the shepherd took her hand. The contact so revolted her that she nearly jumped back. How sordid her longings now seemed!

She arrived home exhausted and with a splitting headache. All that remained of their outing was torment and depression.

"An old man!... An old man with one foot in the grave!"

XV. The Fall

Mila's feet once again rested firmly on the ground. Fallen from the nest of her illusions, she found herself face to face with reality. The vague dreams, hopes and fears that had bedeviled her were gone, and the shock she had received on Highpeak left her feeling disoriented. As time passed, perplexity gave way to flat, calm resignation. The day after Gaietà's and Baldiret's departure, Mila cleaned the hermitage, which she had neglected since the beginning of her illness, and after dusting, mending, and weeding the garden, she set out to buy food in Murons. On her way she stopped at St. Pontius' Farm, where she had not been seen for many weeks.

It was nearly eleven, and as she approached she spied Arnau unhitching the wagon. The two of them had not spoken since that day in the yard, and he looked less robust. At first he didn't notice Mila, and when he finally saw her a few feet away, he quickly turned and bent over as though to search for something on the ground. She stopped for a moment, disconcerted. Then, understanding that he hoped thus to avoid her, she sadly entered the house, where another unpleasant surprise awaited her. Seated as usual by the fire, the grandmother was slicing something into a casserole that lay at her feet. Bright flames from a pile of logs filled the hearth and outlined her figure in red. A dark gray cat rubbed against her skirts, sniffing and meowing.

"Good morning, granny! How've you been?" Mila asked cheerfully as she entered.

The old woman, who was bent over, glanced toward the door without removing her hands from the casserole.

"Oh, it's you!" she mumbled and returned to her work as though nothing had happened.

Mila stopped in her tracks. She had expected a warmer welcome from the grandmother, who had always been the kindest member of that family. But as the old lady was known to be temperamental, Mila thought she was in a bad humor or perhaps angry at her for not visiting more often. She therefore approached her, laughed nervously, and tapped her on the shoulder.

"Well, how've you been keeping since the last time I saw you?"

"Right now, thank God... I've never been worse!..." she answered without raising her head.

"I've missed you...," Mila added, not knowing what else to say.

An unpleasant croak, meant as a sarcastic laugh, preceded the old woman's reply: "I bet! Well, let's not talk about that..."

Mila saw that she was in the way and awkwardly excused herself. When she was outside, her chin trembled as she held back the tears. What was going on there? Why had they treated her so coldly? She could understand Arnau's reaction: rightly or wrongly, he was probably still hurt, but the grandmother? She couldn't imagine what the old lady might have against her.

"She's just in a bad mood!" she finally decided. But feeling unsure of her explanation, she visited them two or three times during the next week. She was quickly convinced that their feelings toward her had changed. Marieta still welcomed her as sweetly as ever, but even she could not hide a certain involuntary reserve. The grandmother and Arnau, however, made no effort to hide their feelings. He turned away and disappeared as soon as he caught sight of her, while the old woman clucked quietly in disapproval if Marieta was present, and otherwise simply turned her back on Mila.

Mila racked her brain, trying to understand why she had fallen from favor in that house. Had they learned that she was a cause of Arnau's broken engagement? Had they heard about Matias' doings?

One day Gaietà took his flock up the mountain and stopped at the hermitage to greet Mila, who couldn't help asking about Marieta and the others.

"Listen, shepherd: what's up with Arnau? Is he getting married or not?"

"Is he getting married? I'll say he is!... Before harvest time we'll have a new young lady at St. Pontius."

"Thank God! Everything's all right!" the woman thought, feeling as though a weight had been lifted from her shoulders, but then what on earth was bothering them? And she told Gaietà how they had behaved in her presence.

"Don't worry about it, hermitess... Did you do something wrong? Well then, keep your chin up... It's just gossip, but sooner or later the truth will out, and then..."

"But why are they acting like that?"

He reluctantly replied: "They're good people at St. Pontius, y'know...but they think I care more about you than them, and..." The shepherd suddenly lost his habitual composure and bitterly exclaimed: "That bastard's got an evil tongue...just wait'll I cut it out!..."

Mila inquired no further. Crushed and astonished, she understood at last. She would never again set foot in St. Pontius!

Fortunately, Baldiret was a child and immune to such suspicions. The first Sunday after he left her, she heard him run across the courtyard and dash up the stairs. She hurried out just as eagerly to welcome him.

When they met, the boy threw his arms around her legs and silently buried his head in her skirts. With tears in her eyes, she led him into the kitchen, where she sat down on the bench with Baldiret at her knee and her arms around him, while the two of them chattered away like a couple of excited songbirds.

"Do you still go out with the flock? How do you like school? Do they tell you bedtime stories? Don't you ever miss me?..."

The boy plucked at her woolen shawl.

"I can do my multiplication tables, y'know? Yesterday a boy couldn't get six times six right, and the teacher whacked him on the back of the head... Grandma wanted me to go to Catechism today...but well, this is the only time I could come and visit you... My mouth gets dry from so much reciting... Our teacher said next month I'll be able to write... But I have a hard time remembering all those words in Castilian..."

Seeing Baldiret scratch his head furiously as he talked, she combed his hair and looked for bugs. Then she gave him candy and toasted almonds she kept for visitors, and a piece of gold trim off a Christ Child he had been eyeing covetously for a while. Since he had been away for a few days, she showed him the flowers on the terrace and the cabbages in the garden, whitened by frost, their dead leaves flattened against the ground... When it was time for the boy to go, she accompanied him most of the way home, and he promised that next Sunday he would tell the same fib and come again.

After those two visits, she spent the days by herself... She had done her very best to make Matias see reason, but she quickly found that it was like talking to the wall. He was lost to her forever. Miraculously cured by that revelation on Highpeak, which had dispelled her stubborn blindness, she saw that her neglect had allowed him to slip beyond her grasp. The new element she had sensed in him had completed its work. The brood hen, the loafer, as Gaietà had put it, had been transformed into a compulsive gambler. Pale and gaunt after sleepless nights, his brow furrowed and his glance shifty, he had the air of a beast furtively wolfing down its prey in some cave, but ready to turn and defend its spoils to the death if need be. She had thought him a born idler, but in fact he was born to gamble, nor would he ever change his ways. His education was complete!

Realizing this, Mila ceased to struggle. All her efforts had been for nought, she was alone in the world, and she could expect no help from anyone or anything... And accepting this state of affairs, she acquired the tempered strength of one who, throwing down his last coin and playing his last card, knows he has nothing left to lose. She had been feeling this way for a couple of weeks when early one afternoon the sky, which had been calm, suddenly clouded over. Luminous white castles appeared above Highpeak and spread across the mountains, blackening till within an hour great thunderclaps burst forth. It was the first big storm since Mila's arrival and, bristling like a cat, she roamed from one window to another.

After a mighty rumble that rolled across the heavens, as though a bass drum were announcing the tempest's arrival, sheets of rain beat against the panes like a shower of gravel. Mila, whose nose was pressed against the bedroom window, saw a gray curtain descend, obliterating the dark silhouette of Roquís Gros. That curtain, shaken by sudden gusts and ripped periodically by bolts of lightning, quickly became impenetrable. Mila ran to the little window in her kitchen. The water poured down Roquís Mitjà's slopes, forming streams as it went, falling upon the house and filling the sink's open gutter, from which it flowed in foamy eddies. The sound was deafening, and the pounding rain on the rooftop was accompanied by howling winds that battered the hermitage, rattling frames, ringing bells in terrified confusion, and whistling down the belfry stairs as though about to invade the house. Calmed and delighted by that tumult, Mila stopped up the kitchen door, beneath which water gushed as from a row of faucets. After mopping the little bedroom, she placed basins in the big one to catch the drops from its leaky ceiling... As she worked, she remembered that she had hung an apron on the balcony outside the sitting room. God knew where it was by now! She hurried to see if it had blown away. Fortunately, she had tied it to the railing. With one broken string, it flapped wildly in the wind, but if she didn't hurry the other would snap as well, and undoubtedly that would be the end of her apron. As soon as she unbolted the doors, a mighty gust that nearly bowled her over smashed them against the walls several times till all the panes were broken. Panting as she tried to catch her breath in the wind, Mila stuck her head and one arm out to untie the apron, but the knot was soaked, while the rain stung her face and she felt a few cold drops trickle down her back. Just then, she heard something rattling.

"Oh my God!" exclaimed the woman. "It's the beggar from Murons!"

The mute beggar at Murons wore a bell around his neck. He often visited the hermitage and was very fond of Mila, who would give him not only a slice of bread but a drink of wine as well.

She hadn't seen him for a long time, and hearing his bell, she thought he must have been caught in the storm.

"Hold on! I'll be down in a second!" she shouted, forgetting that the man could no more hear than speak, and re-entering the hermitage, she grabbed one of Matias' mufflers, wrapped it around her neck, and returned to the balcony, where she again struggled to untie the apron. With a great effort, she managed to lean over the railing and glance around. The beggar was nowhere to be seen.

"Oh dear!" she mumbled. "I was sure that was him."
And after loosening the apron, she stepped back to the
door and immediately heard the hollow tinkling again,
louder, more distinct, and seeming to come from the sky.
She broke out in a cold sweat, her grip loosened, and the
apron flew away. Then she feebly bolted the doors, held
onto the walls as she crossed the sitting room, found
some matches in the kitchen, and after entering the little
bedroom, made her way down the steps to St. Pontius'
chapel. It was flooded too, but she hardly noticed. She lit
two candles on the altar, fell to her knees, and opened
her arms before the blessed saint's portrait.

"Oh St. Pontius! Don't let him be hurt! Don't let them
catch him! Spare me this shame!" And writhing like an
epileptic, she fell upon the presbytery stairs.

On the shepherd's last visit, they had discussed Matias,
and the old man, shaking his head, had said things looked
bad for her husband.

"People in town have been complaining... Orders have
come down, and a trap's been set and baited. If they
don't stop gambling – and I'm sure they won't – you can
bet your last penny they'll all wind up in jail...and your
husband'll be the first to go. He's the most reckless, since
he usually wins, and he hangs around there every day and
every night."

Mila, who had grown indifferent to Matias' fate, had
paid little attention to the old man's words, but now,
hearing that strange clanking on Highpeak, it was as
though his prediction fell upon her like the wrath of God.
Because she was certain that it was the skeleton and that
the trouble would be hers as well.

Her tearful eyes again looked prayerfully toward St.
Pontius, while she begged: "Don't let him be hurt!...
Don't let them catch him!"

Never had she felt such pure devotion, and in apology
for asking the saint to help one who had robbed him, she

explained that Matias was her husband, that he was foolish but not wicked, that their fates were linked and the shame would be theirs to share... They would be thrown out of the hermitage. What would they do without money, shelter, or anywhere to go?

He would keep gambling in a corner of some tavern, but what of her?... And again she pleaded: "Don't let them catch him! Don't let them catch Matias! If you must punish him, make him sick or something that won't shame us!"

She left the chapel holding one of those candles. It was barely four o'clock, but night had already fallen. The thunder still rumbled, the wind still howled and bellowed, the sound of rushing water came from all sides, and green lightning bolts occasionally rent the darkness. But when, after supper, the woman crawled into bed, the storm seemed to recede slowly, like a devastating army, leaving behind a mixture of real and imagined noises. Thus the familiar sounds of the Roar, the owl in the belfry, and the grandfather clock mingled with the hoarse whispers of streams, distant barks and plaintive bleats...a turbulent blend of echoes that troubled her sleep.

She woke with a single idea: to find out what had happened and set her mind at rest. And if she arrived in time, to talk with Matias, tell him of the mountain's warning, and try to frighten him into abandoning his evil ways. Mila knew he slept at Anima's lair, and there she hoped to find him.

She decided to feed the rabbits first. Outside the door, she tripped over a big branch from the cypress. The cisterns were full of greenish water in which twigs and snails floated. The steps down to the terraces were covered with debris, the tilled earth had been washed away, and the almond trees were surrounded by tiny buds... The storm had ravaged everything like a second St. Pontius' festival.

"More hard luck!" thought the woman and, wishing to see no more, she took her basket and set off for Murons.

The sky was calm and clear, but the earth still bore the signs of that furious onslaught. At every step Mila found new puddles, gullies, heaps of mud and rocks, uprooted kermes oaks, hitherto unknown springs. And further down, toward the tilled fields, olive groves strewn with branches, as though someone had shaken them from every single tree... Badblood Creek was swifter and more perilous than ever and, overflowing its narrow bed beneath Pont del Cop, it left a coat of black slime upon the banks on either side.

When Mila caught sight of St. Pontius' Farm, her chest suddenly tightened and she recalled her quarrel with its inhabitants. She felt as innocent as a newborn babe, yet they considered her a loose woman. And now, mulling over what had occurred, Mila wondered if the grandmother, a decrepit mummy condemned to sit all day before the fire, hated not her supposed wickedness but her youth and beauty, while Arnau, whom she had unknowingly captivated and subdued, could not forget that she had spurned him for another...

"What a petty, mean-spirited bunch!"

Mila bitterly decided to cross the foot bridge without stopping, but as she approached it, she heard someone calling her from the garden. Surprised, she turned around. Marieta ran toward her, waving a kerchief and shouting: "Wait for me! I'll come with you!"

Mila halted, feeling even more astonished. When they were together, Marieta tied the kerchief around her head and exclaimed, without even bothering to say good morning: "Who would have imagined! We were sure he was at the hermitage!"

The woman seemed very excited. Mila, who understood nothing, continued to stare at her.

"But when the dog showed up, barking and scratching

at the door, we knew something was wrong. He was covered with mud, and as soon as we opened it he ran toward the bridge, looking back and barking. And since we just stood there, he ran back and forth like he wanted us to follow him. 'If Mussol's come to fetch us, something must be wrong,' my husband said, so he and Arnau took the shotgun and followed the dog... Then they went for the police, and now they've all gone back to get him."

"To get who?" squeaked Mila, finally recovering her voice.

Marieta looked at her in amazement: "Oh my God! The shepherd, of course!" and seeing Mila's eyes grow wider, she asked: "Didn't you know?"

Mila barely managed to shake her head.

"Yes, he fell! The shepherd!... He fell from the Flagstones!"

The blood drained from Mila's lips, her legs grew weak beneath her, and she leaned back against the hedge beside the path. The memory of that skeleton on Highpeak drifted across her mind like a thick fog.

Marieta murmured: "I thought you knew! Everyone knows about it...," but at the sight of Mila's drooping head, she gave her a sharp slap.

"I'm sorry," said Marieta. "I was afraid you were going to faint..."

"I had no idea!" Mila replied with a shudder.

Then they set off for the Flagstones, and as they walked Marieta explained what had occurred.

"He must have been making for Lookout Mountain, and when the storm broke he wanted to keep his sheep dry, so instead of going around the long way, he decided to cut across... But the Flagstones were wet and you know how steep they are... The poor man took a fall, head first...and broke every bone in his body..."

Mila managed to ask: "And...is he in bad shape?"

"Bad shape? He's dead, woman, dead!"

Mila gripped Marieta's arm.

"Dead?"

"He was already stiff by the time my husband found him. That's why they went for the police... May he rest in peace, poor shepherd! The dog was acting so crazy they finally had to shoot him. He wouldn't let anyone near the body. And they rounded up the sheep, which were scattered all over..."

Mila then recalled those distant howls and bleats she had heard in her sleep. And she told Marieta about the rattling bones.

"It was a warning, it was a warning!" the woman assured her.

Mila stared at the ground, thinking: "Just a few days ago he was telling me about the skeleton, but who would have thought he'd be the next to go! That was no fairy tale. It all came true... It all came true."

And she had worried about Matias! Well, she could stop worrying now... But why had she thought only of him, as though no one else existed? How strange! And Mila, who still was not herself, began to feel guilty. She should have prayed for the shepherd too. Perhaps she could have saved him!

Before reaching the path that led to the Flagstones, they heard voices and saw a group of people walking toward them. It was the delegation that had gone to fetch the corpse: the judge, the mayor, two doctors and the rector, all from Murons, along with assorted curious onlookers. Behind them, a policeman and Marieta's husband bore a stretcher covered with Gaietà's dark gray cape.

Upon reaching a flat spot, the men laid the stretcher down and stopped to rest. The two women approached them.

"Good morning," said Marieta.

"Good morning," everyone replied.

Mila, whose legs were still unsteady, was unable to utter a word.

The body beneath the cape resembled a mountain range with an occasional peak here and there. The soaked cape looked even darker and was covered with mud.

People milled about, speaking in whispers as though they were in church.

Mila heard a question: "What town was he from?"

"I don't know...from the mountains... The certificate should say..."

She raised her eyes and saw Arnau staring at her, his lips curled in a savage smirk. It pained her to see him rejoice in the shepherd's death, but almost immediately she felt something warm in her hand and saw Baldiret beside her, his face red and his eyes swollen. He clutched her arm, gazed at her, and then gazed at the stretcher.

"You..., he's..." and he let out an anguished wail. A stern glance from his father cut his explosion short.

Hearing that Gaietà was dead, the boy had run to the Flagstones, where they had found him sobbing inconsolably. Only his father's threats had silenced him at last, and lest he be sent to his room, he tried to control himself.

Mila stroked his head and kissed him.

Marieta slowly asked her husband: "Aren't you going to let the boy see him?"

"Go ahead, show him," ordered the judge, who had overheard their conversation.

Everyone approached the stretcher.

Marieta's husband lifted the cape, exposing the old man's face.

Mila felt the tears run down her cheeks.

Like the cape, like his clothes, his face was caked with mud. He was almost unrecognizable. His cheeks were green and sunken, his brow was dull white, like lard, and his eyes, though open, were glazed, reminding Mila of that hare they had skinned on the mountain. There was a purplish bump above his left eye – from his fall, no doubt – and patches of blood still clung to his hair. Could that motionless figure really be the shepherd?

She wondered with the same incredulity she had felt beholding the sea. At a signal from the judge, the men covered the corpse and picked up the stretcher, while the onlookers all set off again for Murons.

"Where are they taking him?" Mila asked.

"To the hospital," someone replied and then stared at her in surprise.

Arnau, who walked ahead of her, turned and spat on the ground.

Mila felt her strength ebbing. When they reached the Pont del Cop, she said goodbye to Marieta.

"Where are you going?"

"Home... I don't feel well...," and after crossing the bridge, she turned onto the path.

Hearing that she was unwell, Baldiret stopped as if to follow her. He looked at Mila, then at the stretcher, and finally ran to overtake the crowd.

194

XVI. Suspicions

With each passing day, Mila became more aware of the shepherd's absence. Her initial reaction had been shock. The way she had found out, her walk with Marieta, that disfigured corpse on the stretcher, motionless, speechless, and sightless – it had all been like a tragedy in which the townspeople played roles that left little room for individual feelings. Her own emotions had been touched, but not very deeply. Even on the morrow, when she attended Gaietà's funeral and joined the crowd bearing his body to its resting place, she was distressed by her own sense of disconnectedness. With untroubled spirit she gazed at everything around her: the women's contorted faces, Marieta's nose, red from crying and the cold weather, Matias' sallow, sleepy visage among the men who walked before her. He had donned that bizarre felt hat and his best black jacket, which, far from being tight, now looked several sizes too big. Her attention flitted from one thing, to another, and she heard the woman on her right say to a friend beside her: "I went to see him in the hospital... His neck was broken and his whole face was crushed!" The other replied: "And his shirt and sash were torn, as if he'd tried to grab onto something." Then the first one added: "Poor man! How can you grab onto a flat rock?" And the other responded: "The doctor said the fall must have killed him instantly..."

The women kept talking, while Mila tried to locate the source of her indifference... Was she really unmoved by the shepherd's demise? Had she never loved that man who had treated her so kindly? "No, no," a voice within her replied. "It's just that all this has nothing to do with Gaietà..." And she imagined him waiting at the door to the hermitage, ready to ask as soon as he saw her: "Well, how was the funeral?" A week later, she still felt the same way and was even less convinced that he was truly dead. She expected him to appear at any moment, asking for something or other.

One day she broke a chain that raised the bolt on the front gates and thought absentmindedly: "I'll ask the shepherd to fix it." Not long thereafter, as she cleaned the wardrobe, she found one of his kerchiefs with Matias' underclothes and mumbled: "Next Sunday I'll take it down to him..." The fact that he was no longer in this world had not really dawned on her. But all the same, she missed his reassuring smile, his sweet laughter, his luminous stories. She felt a vague longing, like the onset of an illness that would weigh more and more heavily upon her grieving spirit.

Her sadness was deepened by the fact that Baldiret no longer visited, as though he too had abruptly passed away. Matias showed up when he wanted something, but being with Matias was the same as being alone. Sitting at one end of the bench with his chin in his hands, he kept his thoughts to himself and seemed half-asleep. Mila, who was tired of her own endless soliloquies, tried to rouse him from his torpor with questions about the world, even if it was the world of that foul tavern where he spent the winter or the sinister passion that slowly consumed him. But Matias didn't feel like talking and offered monosyllabic answers... It was as though he had forgotten how to speak and could not even recall the lies and tall tales he had always favored... It was torture for the woman. Restless and bored, she longed to see people, to hear their voices... One day she resolved to visit St. Pontius'

Farm. She had not been there since the shepherd's funeral, but the cause of their quarrel had vanished with his death. After all, he was as dead for them as for her..., so perhaps now they would treat her a little better. Before setting out, she went to fetch something from the terrace and noticed a black figure among the pines near the Roar.

"Oh dear!" she thought. "It's some woman all by herself!" But then she looked more closely: "No, it's a priest... My God, it's the rector!"

So much for her visit! She hurried back inside and, after spreading a white cloth on the table, she brought out a salami, chocolates, and a plate of cookies. Then she smoothed her skirts and waited. An hour passed, and another, but there was no sign of the rector. Mila kept going out on the terrace. "Why's he taking so long? It's not that far from the Roar!" She even walked halfway down the hill to meet him. In vain: the rector had vanished without a trace. The woman felt snubbed. To walk to the Roar and not stop at the hermitage! What a wasted afternoon!

The next morning she visited St. Pontius. The men were out working, Baldiret was at school, and the grandmother was sick in bed. Mila was delighted to find Marieta alone.

She was mending clothes in the sunlight that streamed through her kitchen window. Her feet rested on a stool, a sewing basket lay beside her, and her glasses were held in place by a band around her kerchiefed head. Marieta's eyesight had deteriorated and she could not sew without her glasses. At Mila's greeting she raised her eyes and looked out over the rusty frames.

"Don't move, Marieta!" Mila cried, and taking another stool, she sat down and asked about everyone in the family. Marieta slowly replied, and Mila learned that Arnau's betrothed had bought a rich hope chest, that

Baldiret was now an altar boy and, since he ate lunch at the rectory, they didn't see him from dawn to dusk, that the grandmother had stones and the doctor said they might have to probe her, that they were worried because their second-born son had been drafted, that Red, the French mare, had given birth to a dead foal... But despite all this information, Mila felt the same reserve as before and sensed that Marieta was not pleased by her visit. Yet she remained seated, as though she were awaiting something, and indeed, that "something" was not long in appearing.

In the course of their conversation Marieta mentioned the shepherd, and Mila, forgetting everything that had occurred, said how much she had missed him in the weeks since his death. Marieta's face suddenly hardened into an expression she had never seen before.

"Come on now! You've got nothing to complain about!"

"What do you mean?" Mila asked in surprise.

"He took care of you two!"

"But his favorite was Baldiret..."

Marieta looked up and exclaimed: "Well, he chose a funny way to show it!" But she quickly calmed herself and added: "I mean, may he rest in peace! Who knows whose fault it was?"

Taken aback by these mysterious words, Mila softly replied: "I don't know what you're talking about, Marieta."

"Come on! Don't play dumb!" And she laughed with the same hardness Mila had seen in her face: "If that was his will, there's nothing I can say... He must have known what he was doing... Everyone has his obligations... What bothers me is that people think we..., including the *senyor* rector, who keeps saying how Gaietà told him this and Gaietà told him that... Well, so what? He told us lots of stuff too, but the fact is we haven't seen a penny."

Mila finally began to understand: Marieta was talking about money.

"God Almighty!" she exclaimed. "Do you think he left us something?"

"I know he didn't make a will, but as far as leaving or... or...whatever you want to call it...the government wants its share of that money!"

"Listen: he didn't leave or give us anything! You say he had money, but we didn't even know that!"

Mila spoke with such conviction that Marieta lowered her eyes. But her voice insisted: "Well, I don't know...but they didn't find it on him, and he couldn't have taken it with him!"

Mila indignantly retorted: "So you figure we must have it!"

Marieta retreated a little: "Now I didn't say that...but people have to pay their debts...and if he owed anything to anyone..."

Then Mila suddenly grasped the woman's train of thought. The shepherd had "paid his debts" – in other words, her favors.

"My God," she moaned, and covering her face, she began to sob.

Marieta hastily put her sewing down on the stool.

"Hey, what's the matter? I mean, what did I say?"

Mila thought: "What a jealous, nasty crew! They were afraid he'd leave us something!... How can they be so stingy and mean?"

And controlling her tears, she proudly replied: "Marieta, I didn't know what you were like...but not even God can forgive what you've said." And rising to her feet, she wiped her eyes and continued: "Just get this through your skull, and may I be struck dead if I'm lying! I never slept with the shepherd! You hear me, Marieta? Never! As far as his money's concerned, God knows what he did with it, but our consciences are as clear as the saints' up in Heaven!"

And she silently approached the door, but Marieta motioned her to stop.

"Don't go out looking like that! Calm down first... What'll people think if they see you?... And besides, where there's smoke there's fire..."

Mila looked at her again.

This time the woman met her gaze: "You owed everyone money, you told me so yourself... Well, if he didn't leave you anything, how come you paid your bills so quickly?"

Mila was more astonished than if a cannon had fired outside the house.

"What? You think we...?" And recovering, she added: "I wish we did!" with a bitter smile.

"Don't tell me you're going to deny that too! The shopkeepers told me!"

Mila opened her mouth to reply, but Marieta cut her off: "Since they didn't find anything on the shepherd, people reckoned you'd have it and made a beeline for your husband, who paid them off right away. So now what do you expect everybody to think? If it wasn't Gaietà, then who gave you all that money?"

Mila felt a wave of pain spread through her body. Why did the Fates pursue her so relentlessly? Why did everything turn out wrong?

She stared at Marieta, her lips trembled as she tried to speak...and suddenly she stuffed her tear-soaked handkerchief between her teeth and bit down as hard as she could.

"Goodbye," she stammered and fled homeward, leaving Marieta staring after her at the door.

She ran all the way back to the hermitage.

Why had Matias paid all their bills at once? Why couldn't he be a little shrewder? And furthermore, why had the shepherd died? Why had he, who loved her so, left her sorrow instead of riches? He had promised that sooner or later the truth would out, but that wasn't what had happened!... She nervously gnawed her hands and tugged at her hair.

Like a wounded beast who crawls off to die, she resolved never again to descend the mountain. Everyone else would be just as spiteful as Marieta! Gossip was like a weed: once it spread, you couldn't uproot it... The people in Murons would all point at her and stare! She wasn't strong enough to bear it. If they had to insult her, let it not be to her face! Let Matias fetch things while she stayed at home, dead to the world.

Her intention was thwarted by Baldiret's arrival two days later. He came not of his own volition but to say the rector wished to see her. Mila anxiously asked the boy if he knew what it was about, and hearing that he did not, she hurriedly took her lunch off the fire and followed him.

The rector was seated in the armchair behind his desk. He invited Mila to come in and shut the door behind her.

"Sit down, hermitess... I sent for you because...because I hoped we could speak together. I nearly visited you a few days ago, but frankly, I couldn't bring myself to enter your house... Some things are difficult...difficult to say. But then yesterday Baldiret's mother spoke to me again..."

Mila, who had paled and stiffened at the mention of Marieta, now sat on the edge of her seat like a prisoner about to be sentenced. What had happened since their conversation? What had the rector heard? She never found out, but she was put through a gruelling interrogation full of leading questions and cruel revelations. In that net of traps and innuendoes, one thing stood out clearly: the shepherd had hidden "money, lots of money" in a belt beneath his sash. He had told the rector of his plan to leave half to the Church, "in memory of the

Mother and Son," and half to Baldiret. The rector had
taken charge of the dead man's body, but no one had
seen either the belt or the money. Matias had recently
paid all his creditors, and if anyone knew where the
money was, he was obliged to speak out or lose his soul,
since to remain silent would be "to rob the Church and
an innocent child," whereas "those who repent will be
forgiven, for Our Lord God is merciful..."

Mila sweated through this long speech, which was
further lengthened by the rector's habitual repetitions,
for despite his insistence that he was merely asking, as
Gaietà had stayed so long at their house, it was obvious
that he shared Marieta's suspicions. Mila denied everything, forgetting her respect for the rector and fiercely
defending herself against his insinuations. A thousand
times no! They knew nothing about the shepherd, had
never seen his money, and she didn't mind repeating it
for all the world to hear! But maybe not everyone else
could say the same!... Maybe those who talked the
loudest had something to hide... In any case, Gaietà had
moved out a while back... Her eyes flashed as she
repeated, with maniacal tenacity, that she was a respec-
table woman, Almighty God was her witness... Till at last
the rector, who had listened attentively and kept his eyes
fixed upon Mila, holding up his hand in an effort to calm
her, said he "considered her a good woman and never
went just by what people said." But when, somewhat
mollified by this declaration, she confessed as another
proof of their innocence that Matias could have won the
money gambling, the rector dropped his hand and looked
at her suspiciously.

"So I'd heard, so I'd heard, and that's why...because
what else can you expect? A gambler's capable of
anything. It's true they've stopped for a while because we
gave them no choice. They were leading others into sin...
But they'll start again, mark my words, it's too late to

save them...and when they do, keep an eye out...anyone can slip and fall...and if you notice...since I know you're a good woman...have no fear...because a priest, a father confessor..."

Mila left the rectory feeling even more depressed than after her conversation with Marieta. God, because of Matias people thought they were thieves, nor was there any way to refute such accusations! The rector had even asked her to spy on her own husband.

Unfortunately, Matias visited her that evening. He slept at home more than before, and she now understood why. He sat silently by the fire and, seeing the troubled look on his face, she thought: "That's why he's been acting stranger and stranger! He's wasting away now that he can't gamble anymore."

She felt like telling him everything, throwing the truth in his face, but why bother? What good could possibly come of it? And besides, as soon as her words sank in, he would start trying to think up lies and excuses.

The woman had long ago learned to keep her thoughts to herself, but this one tipped the scales.

She had gradually relinquished all her feelings for Matias: first consideration, then affection, then patience and now resignation. What remained was a bitter scorn that within a day turned to fury. His footsteps, his face, his voice, and even his breathing were so hateful that she could barely control herself. During the day, when he was out or she was busy around the house, it wasn't so bad, but at night in their bed her torment seemed unbearable. The slightest contact made her start and instinctively pull away, covering her ears so as not to hear his snoring.

He no longer enjoyed the untroubled sleep of a peaceful brute but turned from side to side, scratching, kicking and whimpering like a beaten child, and at each movement she thought: "He's going to wake up!" Revolted, she pulled away till she nearly fell off the bed and then lay still, scarcely daring to breathe lest she rouse him...till at the first cracks of daylight around the shutters, she leapt up, took her clothes, and dressed in the kitchen.

Her decline was as precipitous as it had been before, and her green eyes swelled till they seemed to devour her face, as they had in Gaietà's story about the Lord of Llisquents.

XVII. That Night

Matias told Mila there was going to be a festival in Murons, and the first evening she went to watch the people dancing. The old square buzzed like a beehive, while well dressed ladies bedecked the balconies, from whose Olympian heights they observed the *sardanas* below them.

Deafened by the uproar, Mila took refuge in an arcade whose square columns, frequently watered by dogs and children, gave off a smell like an open sewer.

On the outside, two or three rows of backs blocked her view, while on the inside a constant stream of merrymakers trod on her skirts and shoved her. Trapped between that human wall before her and the river at her back, her nose assaulted by the piercing stench of urine, Mila felt bored and uncomfortable. Was this supposed to be fun? If she couldn't see anything, she might as well go where the air was fresher and there was less commotion. And making her way through the crowd, she decided to buy a few things and return home.

At the top of France Street she met the musicians, who were on their way to have a drink during intermission. It was the same band that had performed at St. Pontius' festival, and the cornetist grinned, gave her a roguish wink, and shouted: "Hello there, beautiful!" His head was shaped like a jug, and Mila couldn't help laughing as she remembered how he had flirted with her at the festival till someone told him she was a married woman. That unexpected encounter dispelled her bad humor, and still thinking about the cornetist's funny face, she completed her purchases and set out for home.

Matias, who had been watching, caught up with her as she left town.

"You leaving already?"

"Yes. Want to come?"

Matias scratched his head.

"Now? It's still early. When they stop dancing...or after supper... There's going to be a torchlight procession."

Mila caught on immediately.

"So of course you want to stay...," she said sarcastically.

"For a while at least..."

"Well then, go ahead," she replied, this time without rancor. And she set off again for the hermitage.

"See you later!" Matias shouted after her, adding when he thought she was out of earshot: "I'll be home late, so don't wait up for me... I'll knock on the gate."

What luck! An evening all to herself! And she cheerfully made her way up the mountain, still thinking of that cornetist.

Only a nice fellow could have a face that made everyone happy, including her. You couldn't look at him without laughing, and if she knew him a hundred years, she'd still smile whenever she saw him. Why had he thought she was single? She didn't act like such a girl, nor did she feel pretty that day. But he didn't care; he was the fun-loving type. What a stroke of luck, having a temperament like that...

And absorbed in such idle musings, she reached the hermitage as the sun went down. She entered the dark sheep shed and groped for eggs in the nests. There were two...three...six, seven... With her hands full she climbed the stairs, entered the little bedroom, and put them in a basket. She counted them. One more and she'd have three dozen to sell. Not bad for a week's work!

She covered the basket and took off her best clothes. Then she closed the balcony doors in the sitting room and went to light the fire and an oil lamp. Supper was ready and only had to be reheated. She went down again to lock the gate outside the courtyard. A cricket was chirruping loudly, and without knowing why, she felt an urge to have snails for supper. "Tomorrow I'll get some," she thought hungrily as she bolted the gates, but when she turned toward the hermitage she gasped. She thought she'd seen something move in the yard. She looked more closely. Bah!... It was nothing! She was still afraid of the dark, just like the shepherd said... All the same, as she climbed the steps she uneasily turned around. God! This time she let out a blood-curdling shriek and dashed for the kitchen door. Whatever had been lurking in the shadows was now right behind her... She hadn't the presence of mind to shut the door as she entered. A man stood on the threshold. Terrified, she stepped back and leaned against the table.

"Don't be afraid," he stammered hoarsely, the whites of his eyes glinting in the lamplight.

If they'd punched a hole in Mila, not one drop of blood would have trickled out. But seeing the man move toward her, she shouted: "What do you want?"

He halted.

"Don't be afraid... *Hoo, hoo, hoo!...*" And sticking his hand in his trousers, he began to search for something.

"I said what do you want!" she repeated, feeling even more frightened.

He swallowed nervously and hesitated.

"*Hoo hoo hoo...* I wanted to ask if you'd..."

His last hoarse syllable died in his throat.

Mila was shaking like a leaf, but with a great effort she managed to reply: "Get out...get out this very minute!"

But he didn't move; he seemed nailed to the spot. He only extended his apelike paw, in whose palm a gold coin glittered.

"What d'you say, eh?" And he threw the coin at her feet, where it rang noisily upon the floor.

The woman backed away till she reached the wall. His eyes glowed like the day she had caught him watching her beneath the almond tree.

"You want two? Take 'em...," he muttered, and another coin struck the floor and rolled under the table.

"No, no!" she screamed. "Get out of my house!"

But instead of leaving, he took another step forward. He breathed heavily through his nose and trembled as though a tarantula had bitten him.

"You want more, eh? Go on, take 'em all!" and handfuls of coins rained down at the woman's feet.

She stood rigid and silent, as though bewitched by that shower of gold. But suddenly her terror roused her and, feeling wings sprout on her heels, she fled toward the bedroom as fast as she could.

She heard him roar with fury and then howl as he pursued her. With Anima close behind and betrayed by her own footsteps, she swiftly vanished down the stairs that led to the chapel, cut across it and even reached the little door behind the altar, but as she turned the knob something tripped her, and she fell upon the flagstones...

Before everything went black, she felt the beast's paws and his hot breath upon her flesh.

After sitting for a long time on the floor, Mila rose to her feet. Everything still seemed hazy, and lights danced before her eyes. She made her way through the sacristy, crossed the storeroom behind it, and pushed open the door that led to the sheep shed. The courtyard was outlined in pale moonlight, and beyond it the gates yawned menacingly. Outside, that cricket was still chirruping away. Mila climbed the steps. On the landing, the kitchen door also stood open: the rectangle of light from the oil lamp within looked like a golden seal upon the whitewashed wall, reminding Mila of those coins that had fallen at her feet.

She entered the kitchen: nothing glittered on the floor. The murderer had gathered his treasure before departing. The only sign of his visit was a wet footprint near the door... Noticing that her hands were sticky, Mila looked down. They were covered with blood, as was her woolen shawl. She lit a candle stub she kept beside the sink and went into the sitting room. There were one...two...three wet footprints on the tiles. She raised her candle and looked at the clock: nearly nine fifteen. Its taunting tick-tock was as steady and persistent as the cricket's chirrups.

She entered her bedroom and approached the mirror. Everything looked red, like clouds tinted by a brilliant sunset. She blinked and looked again: her face, like her hands and shawl, was covered with blood, and there was a gash that ran from her cheekbone to her chin. Now she understood why the fall had been so painful. Her head must have struck an iron bolt on that old altarpiece in the sacristy... She washed the cut with alcohol, which brought tears to her eyes. Afraid of fainting, she stopped and looked in the mirror. Though the cut was not deep, she would bear the scar all her life.

She put on another shawl and washed her hands. Something seemed to draw her out of the hermitage. She snuffed out the candle and crossed the sitting room. The night was mild and so bright that she could see the sundial's round face on the kitchen wall, where it grinned like that flirtatious cornetist in Murons. The front gates beckoned her and she went outside. The firmament swirled above her, sprinkled with stars in whose brilliant light everything seemed to glow.

Mila calmly sat down upon a rock on the hillside. She, who had been so anxious, had suddenly lost her fear.

What else could possibly happen? With her legs together and one elbow resting on her knee, she held her kerchief against the wound on her face.

In the distance she spied Roquís Gros, a dark and starless patch of sky, and further down, vague forms swam in a grayish penumbra, from which a deep hush full of inaudible harmonies rose like smoke from a censer. Mila happily wrapped herself in that awesome stillness. She knew that any sound would cause her an almost physical pain, and she thanked the stubborn cricket, who had now fallen silent. Maybe she had squashed it as she passed through the gate... And she thought: who knows if it's a sin to kill a cricket? Crickets are alive, and even a cricket's life is real. To kill it before its time is the worst it can suffer, because like all living beings, a cricket has but one life... Only one: that's not much!... And if we idly destroy it? If it's crushed like that cricket? Was there no possible atonement? Perhaps it was a sin to kill a cricket, a greater sin than many she had thought dreadful...

Sin was something that had always puzzled Mila, and now, as she reconsidered it, her thoughts seemed to rise into the celestial vault. And she, at the center of a thought that embraced the world, quickly grasped what she had failed to understand and saw the dark side of everything with such clarity that she crossed herself in thanks for her restored vision. For example: how could she not have noticed that Anima was after her? How could she have misunderstood the way he looked at her the day they met, when she was busily polishing that candleholder in the chapel? She recalled the way he had stared, as though dazzled by her presence; now she saw the lust in those sunken eyes. And furthermore, every time she had run across him, his actions had pronounced the same ugly prophesy. Gaietà had said: "You've got nothing to worry about as long as I'm alive..." But why hadn't she seen that Anima, who like her had misconstrued the shepherd's feelings, would first get rid of him and then fall upon her... Because both she and Anima had been entirely mistaken. Gaietà had never loved her as a man loves a woman. It was not his age, his amulet, or his virtue that stood between them. No, it had been a memory, a shadow, a respect for his beloved wife, the servant girl at St. Pontius.

Now, in the new clarity that suffused all her thoughts, she saw them walking together, one dead and the other living. Now she felt the unbreakable bond that held their souls together.

A long screech from the belfry owl interrupted her meditations, seeming to rend the air as that iron bolt had torn her face. Perhaps the air would bear a mark like the one on her cheek. She felt the world must be full of such signs...

She sat up without taking her hand from her face. The flesh on her knee was red from her elbow. She placed her other hand beneath it and sat still as if paralyzed.

The night enfolded Mila in its innumerable veils, but she remained unaware, her attention focused on her hurt knee and knotted stomach.

The moon had risen, bathing everything in its aqueous blue-green light: the cisterns like colossal emeralds, those two cypresses, taller than ever, embracing like two old giants about to bid each other farewell, Roquís Gros, dark blue against the sky's uncertain glow, which seemed to ring the mountain like a mysterious aureole about its buried legends, the kitchen's cold white wall, and pine groves, hillsides, cliffs and distances all dissolving in that silent, shoreless sea.

A big night bird swooped noisily overhead, and almost simultaneously a shooting star inscribed its arc upon the firmament, falling to earth not far from the Nina. Mila thought, "The shepherd would have made up a story about that bird and that star... What a wise man he was!

It was as if Dawnflower had given him the wisdom she had promised that old man... Yes, Gaietà always knew what was going to happen..."

And she remembered all the times he had warned her, with furrowed brow, "Watch out for him, hermitess... He's the nastiest character in these mountains..." And later, "That bird of ill omen is circling round your home..." And later still: "I have to look sharp, 'cause if he caught me he'd make me pay for it..." Mila had always laughed at his fears; only now did she realize how justified they were, now that it was too late for her or Gaietà. Because Anima had killed him; she was as sure as if she'd seen it: those pieces of gold ringing at her feet had been the murderer's confession... And she remembered snatches of conversation at Gaietà's funeral: "His neck was broken and his whole face was crushed...his shirt and sash were torn as if he'd tried to grab onto something...covered with blood...his belt was gone." His belt was gone! No, Gaietà hadn't fallen; she knew how careful he always was... He hadn't fallen; someone had pushed him from behind... From behind: he himself had seen it coming. "He's always been as terrified of me as Satan is of crosses, and he's never even dared to look me in the eye..." Anima had crept up behind Gaietà once before and shot at him on Goblin Crest. Like a beast who kills by stealth, he had pushed him down the Flagstones. "How can you grab onto a flat rock?" That's why the shepherd's face had been caked with mud... "The fall must have killed him instantly," the doctor had said... And once he was dead, it was easy to take his belt... Poor shepherd! How could people be so blind? Everyone said, "He took a fall," and they left it at that...while Anima went free and was king of the mountain. Till he met another shepherd and another hermitess.

The woman shuddered, feeling her entrails burn more furiously than her face when she had rubbed it with alcohol. And suddenly, to her horror, another memory returned: her silent prayer at the Roar as she drank its magic waters, and that dream of the saint laughing so hard his fat lady's belly shook... St. Pontius had always hated her! She closed her eyes and drew her legs more tightly together.

Near the cisterns that cricket had begun to chirrup again, dauntlessly repeating his single note, as sour and piercing as a bugle.

She turned around, vainly trying to peer into the blue shadows. She hadn't crushed it... Thank God! Was it really alive?

But her thoughts returned to the shepherd. Those who had been dead for centuries survived in his tales. The world seethed with spectral presences that wandered between Heaven and earth, bereft of the flesh and blood that had once made them visible but even so, still secretly mingling with the living...

And as she remembered, she imagined a will-o'-the-wisp flickering across the hillside below her. She saw that old man among the mocking fairies, condemned to pine eternally for a love that could never be. And then she heard, still further down, the muffled sound of dead voices, the groans of severed heads knocking against the Pont del Cop, turning over and over in the foamy red stream... All Gaietà's tales were about the strange persistence of what had once existed. But they were merely stories invented to amuse and beguile, and Mila's skeptical mind refused to credit what her senses could not perceive...till she ran up against his last one: the skeleton on Highpeak.

Was that just another tale? No it wasn't... During the storm, she had heard those bones rattling above her, and every time she remembered she heard them again... No, that was no story... Well then? Perplexed, Mila gazed down at the shadowy sea below her, as if hoping to dull the brightness of her newly awakened thoughts, which had already begun to fade little by little.

Meanwhile, the moon cast its silver rays over everything, like the webs spiders subtly spin to adorn lonely silences that no man should trouble with his wretched chimeras.

XVIII. The Descent

The imperturbable hours slowly flowed over Mila, who sat motionless upon her rock on the hillside.

Though the night had grown chilly, she never thought of entering the hermitage. On the contrary, whenever her gaze fell upon it, she quickly shuddered and glanced away.

What was she doing there? She was waiting for Matias, who had promised to return that night. "I'll be home late," he had said, and Mila knew why...he was gambling. There was a festival in Murons, and people always gambled at festivals, so there was no danger of his leaving until the game was over, but once it was he would return. She was certain of this fact, and therefore she decided to stay where she was.

She waited as the night inched indifferently toward morning till at last she heard his footsteps echo below her and caught sight of his shadowy figure, barely visible in the pale dawn.

He climbed hurriedly, with lowered head, mulling over something – perhaps some excuse to explain his long night in the village. As soon as he looked up at the hermitage, she called out to him in a casual voice. He stopped, surprised, and gazed all around. Seeing her, he approached uneasily. His weary face was as green as Anima's.

"What? Up so early?"

"I didn't go to bed."

And then, without tears, shouts, or gestures, she told

him everything that had occurred. Her recital was as concise as an inscription on a tombstone, and her green eyes were as calm as a deep, mysterious gorge.

When she had finished, Matias' face revealed the greatest shock he had ever suffered: a cruel, mute expression of fear and consternation.

Seeing him remain silent, she pointed to the hermitage: "Well, after all that, you can be sure I'm not going back, but I didn't want to leave without telling you first."

His corpselike face scowled as he took in these words.

"What?" he mumbled glumly. "You want to go away? Where to?"

She angrily replied: "I don't care... Anywhere... As far away as I can get!"

Like Anima a few hours earlier, Matias began to tremble. For a second, it seemed he would plead or argue, but, unable to summon the will, he quietly submitted, lowering his head and muttering: "Well, let's go then."

But at that moment the gorge suddenly lost its calm, and something furious, demoniacal glowed in the woman's eyes: "Not with you...never again... Don't try to follow me...or I'll kill you."

She stared into his eyes, trying to impress her threat upon his soul.

Then she silently rose and, without looking back, bearing nothing more than the clothes she was wearing, stiffly and solemnly made her way down the slope.

Her destiny had crystallized in that cruel mountain solitude.

216

About the Translator: David H. Rosenthal holds a Ph.D. in comparative literature and has lived for five years in Catalonia. His published translations of Catalan literature include Joanot Martorell's *Tirant lo Blanc*, Joan Perucho's *Natural History*, Mercè Rodoreda's *My Christina and Other Stories* and *The Time of the Doves*, J.V. Foix's *When I Sleep, Then I See Clearly* and two anthologies of modern Catalan poetry. In addition, he is a poet, a jazz and literary critic, and a journalist.

For a list of current titles in hardcover and paperback from Readers International please contact our North American office at P.O. Box 959, Columbia LA 71418-0959 USA or our UK office at 8 Strathray Gardens, London NW3 4NY England.